The Nettlefold Chronicles

Clean Regency Romance

To Wed an Earl

Arietta Richmond

Dreamstone Publishing © 2019 - 2021

www.dreamstonepublishing.com

ISBN-13: 978-1-925165-09-8

Disclaimer

This is a work of fiction. Names, characters, places, organisations, events, and incidents are either products of the author's imagination or used fictitiously.

Dedication

For everyone who had the grace to be patient while this book, and every other book that I have written, was coming into existence, who provided cups of tea, and food, when the writing would not let me go, and endured countless times being asked for opinions.

For the readers who inspire me to continue writing, by buying my books! Especially for those of you who have taken the time to email me, or to leave reviews, and tell me what you love about my books, and what you'd like to see more of – thank you – I'm listening. I hope that you enjoy this new series (which features some appearances by old favourite characters from the His Majesty's Hounds series), just as much as my other books.

For my growing team of beta readers and advance reviewers – it's thanks to you that others can enjoy these books in the best presentation possible!

And for all the writers of Regency Historical Romance, whose books I read, who inspired me to write in this fascinating period.

Introduction

I hope that you enjoy this story. Whilst it can be read standalone, it is related to stories from eight other authors, all of which are in some way related to the area surrounding the town of Upper Nettlefold, and its companion town of Lower Nettlefold. Upper Nettlefold, and its inhabitants have been created by all of us, to share.

This is my fifth visit to Upper and Lower Nettlefold, but it won't be the last. You will almost certainly see other books from the various authors, based in Upper and Lower Nettlefold, or about characters you first meet here. Keep an eye out for books with the Nettlefold Chronicles logo on them!

Every time you read another Nettlefold story, you'll find that it has things which happen, that influence the other stories, or are seen in other stories, from a different perspective. You will find that each story builds on the ones before, weaving the magic of community and interconnection between characters.

There is also a map of Upper Nettlefold, which you will find on the next page, to help you visualise everything, as you read. (Sorry, you'll have to turn the book sideways to see it best)

Although each story can stand alone, we're sure that you'll love finding the linkages as you go.

Arietta Richmond

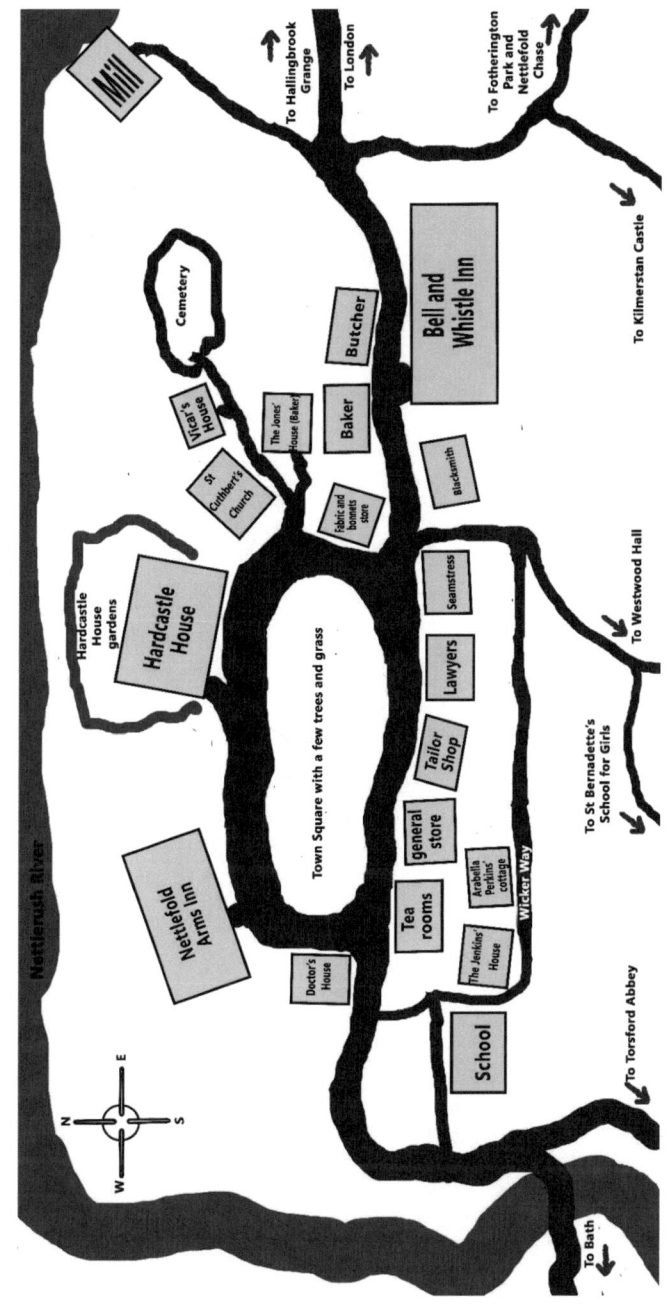

Table of Contents

Books by Arietta Richmond

His Majesty's Hounds

Claiming the Heart of a Duke

Giving a Heart of Lace

Enchanting the Duke

Finding the Duke's Heir

Healing Lord Barton

Loving the Bitter Baron

Rescuing the Countess

Attracting the Spymaster

Intriguing the Viscount

Being Lady Harriet's Hero

Redeeming the Marquess

Winning the Merchant Earl

Kissing the Duke of Hearts

Falling for the Earl

Betting on a Lady's Heart

Courting a Spinster for Christmas

Restoring the Earl's Honour

A Scandalous Spring (An additional short story)

The Scent of First Love (an additional short story)

From Soldier Spy to Lord (contains the first three books in one volume)

To Love a Determined Lady (Contains Books 4, 5 and 6 in one volume)

Love Heals a Lord (Contains Books 7, 8 and 9 in one volume)

To Love a Dashing Lord (Contains Books 10, 11, 12, and 13 in one volume)

For a Lady's Honour (Contains Books 14, 15, 16, and 17 in one volume)

A Duke's Daughters – The Elbury Bouquet

A Spinster for a Spy (Lily)

A Bluestocking for a Baron (Rose)

A Minx for a Merchant (Primrose)

A Vixen for a Viscount (Hyacinth)

A Diamond for a Duke (Camellia)

An Enchantress for an Earl (Violet)

A Maiden for a Marquess (Iris)

A Heart for an Heir (Thorne) (coming soon)

The Family Sagas Collections

The Barrington Saga

The Morton Saga

The Dartworth Saga

The Edgeworth Saga

The Windemere Saga

The Chester Saga

The Nettlefold Chronicles

The Duke and the Spinster

A Duke in Autumn

To Wed an Earl

To Dance with the Dangerous Duke

A Christmas Bride for the Duke

The Marquess Elopes (Coming Soon)

The Scandalous Countess (Coming Soon)

Lady Canterford's Conspirators (The Mayfair Ladies Poetry Society)

A six book series (coming soon)

The Regency Gothic Series

Lord of the Storm   Lord of the Darkness

Lord of the Lost (coming soon)   Lord of the Shadows

The Regency Scandals Series

The Gift of a Christmas Scandal

Lady Mariel's Scandalous Love

Christmas with *That* Duke

Lord of Dragons (written with Kyrii Rayne)

The Derbyshire Set

A Gift of Love (Prequel short story)   A Devil's Bargain (Prequel short story - coming soon)

The Earl's Unexpected Bride   The Captain's Compromised Heiress

The Viscount's Unsuitable Affair   The Count's Impetuous Seduction

The Rake's Unlikely Redemption   The Marquess' Scandalous Mistress

The Marchioness' Second Chance   A Viscount's Reluctant Passion

Lady Theodora's Christmas Wish

A Remembered Face (Bonus short story – coming soon)

The Duke's Improper Love (coming soon)

A Gentleman's Unconventional Courtship (coming soon)

The Derbyshire Set, Omnibus Edition, Volume 1 (the first three books in one volume.)

The Derbyshire Set, Omnibus Edition, Volume 2 (the second three books in one volume.)

Themed Collections

The Regency Christmas Hearts Collection

The Regency Spring and Valentine's Hearts Collection

The Regency Summer Hearts Collection

The Regency Autumn Hearts Collection

The Regency Christmas Love Collection

The Regency Spring Love Collection

The Regency Summer Love collection

Other Books

The Scottish Governess   The Duke's Christmas Vow

Her Summer Duke   Her Passionate Duke

Her Absent Duke   Her Determined Duke

Her Generous Duke   Her Christmas Duke

Lady Augusta's Letters

The Crew of the Seadragon's Soul Series, (coming soon - a set of 10 linked novels)

Prologue

Early 1796

"I will not allow you to demean yourself, Eleanor. How could you think to shame this family so? To suggest that you, the daughter of an Earl, should marry a man whose highest possibility in life is to be the Vicar of a country parish! The thought is not to be borne. And so I told him, when he came to ask me for permission – so presumptuous of him. I sent him away with my stern denial, and you shall not see him again. To make sure of that, I have purchased him a living which is some days' travel from here, in a village with a run-down church and a need of pastoral care. At least there he might do some good in the world."

Lady Eleanor Debenham gasped and brushed at the tears which ran down her cheeks.

"But father... I love him! Surely you can see..."

"I can see very well that you are a foolish girl with no respect for her family or station in life. You will not say another word on this. Instead, in four weeks' time, you will marry the Duke of Walemount, and be grateful for your place in the world."

1

"But father, the Duke is nearing seventy! I cannot marry him, I cannot!"

"You will. And that is my last word on the matter."

Knowing that her father would not relent, Lady Eleanor fled the room. She would be forced to marry the Duke, she had to accept that – but the Duke was an old man... perhaps she would not have to suffer his attentions for too long? And should the time come that she was free again... It was the only hope she might cling to, in the face of her father's cruelty.

*****

Mid 1797

The Duchess of Walemount watched as the casket containing the earthly remains of her late husband was ceremoniously carried into the family crypt, to lie beside the last remains of his two previous wives, and of the Dukes of Walemount who had preceded him. The black veil which covered her face was a blessed disguise, hiding her face from all of the sanctimonious mourners who stood nearby.

When the Duke had lived, they had all called often, currying his favour. And they had all, to a body, resented her existence – for many of them had hoped that he would marry one of their daughters. Now, she might hope that, with his passing, she would not ever have to entertain them again. The new Duke, a son from Walemount's first marriage, was already wed himself, and with two quite young sons of his own, so there was little reason for the toadies to call. And regardless, Eleanor fully intended to remove herself to the Dower House at the earliest opportunity.

From there, she might secretly pursue certain enquiries, whilst praying that her hope was not in vain.

The pall bearers stepped back out into the warmth of the sun, and the crypt door was closed with a resounding and final thud.

She turned away, ignoring those few who might attempt to speak to her, and went to her waiting carriage.

Once settled on the squabs, Eleanor lifted the dark veil with a sigh of some relief and reached out to her maid, who had remained quietly in the carriage the whole time.

"I would hold my daughter, Maggie. I feel the need to touch warmth and unconditional love, after enduring the gaze of all of them…" The nursemaid handed over the swaddled baby, who woke at the movement, and made happy gurgling noises at her mother. "There, my darling, that's right – be happy, for that is what matters most in this world. And if I possibly can, I will make sure that you have the chance to grow up with that happiness, always."

The baby laughed again, her blue eyes sparkling in innocent joy, and Eleanor hardened her resolve even more – she would not let her daughter down.

Early 1798

When a small but elegant carriage drew up before the church of St Stephen in the village of Lower Nettlefold, a cluster of villagers soon appeared at the end of the lane, deeply curious to see who it was – for they recognised the carriages of all of the local aristocracy, and their most frequent visitors. This carriage, they had never seen before.

The carriage door opened, and a Lady stepped down, followed by a maid who carried a small child. It was obvious that the woman was of the Quality, by her clothes and her manner.

But just why she was there was a mystery. She went into the church, followed by the maid, and the onlookers wandered off, hoping that later, they might discover more.

Inside the church, there was silence, and Eleanor looked about in some dismay, for it was obvious that the church was in dire need of some repair, but then, the door to the vestry opened, and a man stepped out, momentarily bathed in the rainbow light which the sun cast through the stained-glass windows, and her breath left her. He stopped, staring, and then his face was transformed by a smile, and her hurried to her, and swept her into his arms. She went, a sob breaking from her lips, and tears starting from her eyes.

"Eleanor! Oh... Your Grace..."

He stepped back, releasing her, looking embarrassed, and she gave a shaky laugh.

"Charles, never call me that."

"But I must, for you are a Duchess! But... why are you here?"

Eleanor took a very deep breath, and mentally cast a prayer to God, begging that her hopes would be answered.

"I am here because my husband has been in his grave these six months and more. It took me some time to discover where you were, and I did not dare to write to you, lest anyone realise my intent, but... I came here in the hope that you might not have married, that you might still care for me... that..."

Her voice broke on the words, and she trailed off into silence, watching his face. For a moment, he looked stunned, as if she had spoken in some other, incomprehensible language, and her heart fell. But then, as his thoughts caught up, he smiled again, and she felt just as weak kneed at the sight as she had two years ago.

"Eleanor... are you saying that you have run away from a life as a Duchess, for me? Are you asking if I still love you?"

"Yes."

4

He laughed, and swept her into his arms, spinning her around, until she laughed too. Then he set her down gently, and brushed a soft kiss over her lips.

"I will always love you, Eleanor. Will you marry me, now that you are free to choose for yourself?"

"Yes, a thousand times yes, Charles. But," and here she turned and waved the maid forward, bringing her to Charles' attention for the first time, "... in marrying me, Charles, you will be taking on a small child too. This is my daughter – Lady Hannah Charteris, if she is to have her full title – and I will not be separated from her!"

Maggie brought the child forward, and Eleanor watched as Charles reached out a gentle finger to brush the child's cheek. At one year old, Hannah was somewhat precocious, but always cheerful. She lifted her tiny hand to his, and gripped his finger firmly.

"Stay?"

Eleanor's heart overflowed at his expression.

"Yes, little Hannah, you can stay. Stay, and I will help your mother raise you, as surely as if you were my own daughter."

*****

Mid 1798

The Earl of Scartmoor regarded the paper in his hand with near apoplectic fury.

How could she have done this to him?

After all that he had done to give her the chance at the highest standing in society, the best situation for the rest of her life! But she had done it, it seemed, and there was no undoing it now.

No undoing her actions – but there was a way that he could respond. He would cut her off completely, so that it was as if she had never existed. It was no more than she deserved. Let her see what life was like without the money for the luxuries she was accustomed to – that would bring home to her just how foolish she had been.

He opened the desk drawer, and brought out a clean sheet of quality paper, then uncapped the inkwell and began to write.

✹✹✹✹✹

Mid 1798

Maria Debenham, Countess of Scartmoor, was pale and worn looking as she sat in the private parlour of her niece, Lady Annabelle Watermain, and her eyes were reddened still from the tears which had fallen. Annabelle watched her with great concern, then reached out to refill her aunt's teacup.

"My dear Aunt, surely he cannot mean it!"

Maria lifted the cup, her hands shaking a little, and sipped the tea before answering.

"He is absolutely serious, my dear. I am so sorry to impose upon you like this – I am not usually such a watering-pot – but I knew not who else I might speak to of this – you have always been so fond of my daughter…. And I cannot discuss this with anyone except the closest of family, for to do so would ensure that gossip would run rife!"

"But… to cast her off utterly! That is beyond the pale – so cruel!"

"It is – but so he has declared it – I am never to see my daughter again, nor mention her. He has changed his will to ensure that she gets nothing. He acts as if she does not exist, as if she has never existed. I cannot bear it! He should not act so – she did his bidding, and now that God has seen

6

fit to release her from that, why should she not do as she wishes? But Francis cannot see it so – all he sees is an insult to the family's status, and he cannot forgive her for it. He will not even show me her letter – he burnt it! – and he will not tell me where she is. If I could, I would seek her out, against his wishes – but I do not know where to start."

She stopped, and sipped the tea again.

Annabelle contemplated her aunt's words, shocked by her uncle's actions, and grieving inside herself. She had, as her aunt had stated, always been fond of her cousin.

"Aunt... I promise you, if I can discover anything of her whereabouts, I will contact her, I will offer what help I can – and if I do find her, I will tell you, somehow, without letting my uncle know of it."

Maria set her cup down, and drew out a linen handkerchief to dab away the last of her tears.

"I am grateful, Annabelle – whatever you may be able to do will be appreciated, I am sure. I am equally grateful for this moment, for your care and gentleness in allowing me to confide in you. But I must go – I have calls to make – the calls which Francis believes to be the entirety of my plans for today. I can only pray that, somehow, I will see my daughter again, in my lifetime."

$$*****$$

1809

Miss Katherine Thompson was beginning to wish that she had never taken the position of Governess to Baron Reville's children. Not only was the Baron intent upon treating her in a most inappropriate manner, but so also was his stepson, she suspected. She was afraid that it was only a matter of time, until one of them caught her alone in a situation where she could not escape.

She did not wish to desert the poor motherless children, but if it came to it, she would leave, to save herself – for, however terrible the lecherous man was to her, he was always kind to his own children. She rose from her bed, and donned her dowdiest gown, before slipping into the nursery, and then the children's bedrooms beyond. Perhaps, by the time she had the children up, dressed, and fed for the morning, the Baron and his stepson would have gone about their business for the day...

Of late, they had been acting rather strangely, spending much time closeted together in the Baron's study, and Katherine suspected that they were planning something – likely something of benefit to no-one but themselves. She just prayed that those plans did not involve her, for if they did, she was sure to be ruined.

In that moment, as the children broke their fast, Katherine made a decision – if she could, she would discover what they planned, before they could act on those plans – and would, if at all possible, not only save herself, but would do whatever it took to ensure that their plans failed. They were quite the most opprobrious gentlemen she had ever met...

✳✳✳✳✳

May 1817

Robert Calthorpe, Earl of Tarynholt, sat with his two closest friends in a private parlour of the Nettlefold Arms Inn. They were dressed in the sombre black of full mourning, and stared into the fire as they made short work of the tankards of ale before them.

"I thank you for your company today. I must admit – I was not at all ready for the strictures of that Will. I cannot believe that he so effectively found a way to keep controlling my life, even from beyond the grave!"

"Now then Calthorpe... I mean, Tarynholt... - that will take some getting used to, still! – surely it's not that bad? I know that we didn't hear the exact wording, not being of the family, but surely..."

Simon Hart, Marquess of Marlby, regarded his friend with some concern – even allowing that Robert had buried his father not a week gone, his expression was one of far greater gloom than Simon had expected.

"It is that bad. Once everyone else had left, I asked Withers if he was sure that the requirement would stand, legally. He assured me that it would."

"That sounds serious, indeed – so, do tell us, what is this onerous requirement that your father has laid upon you?"

Philip Ashton, Earl of Riverford, spoke quietly. He had some sympathy for his friend, being not all that long come into his own title, and remembering the utter dislocation of his life which had been wrought, the moment of his father's death.

Robert took another deep draught of ale, and set his tankard down.

"It is devastatingly simple, and thereby inescapable. You know that my father was mostly an astute man, and as a result, Tarynholt is wealthy – but a great deal of that wealth is in properties which are not entailed. By a large margin, the entailed properties are the ones which require the greatest upkeep, and return the least profit from the farmland."

Simon frowned at him.

"But what has that to do with a difficulty caused by the Will?"

Robert gave a somewhat bitter laugh.

"He's made one single requirement, and if I fail to meet it, I'll lose everything which isn't entailed – it will all go to my rather reprehensible cousin, Herbert. And without those other properties, and the monies which are held in the bank, I'll be tantamount to a titled pauper."

Philip and Simon paled.

"I say, that's rather extreme of him, isn't it? But I suppose he didn't care – after all, being dead, he won't suffer from the privations that such a situation would cause."

"Exactly, Simon. All he cared about was getting his way."

Philip took a mouthful of ale then asked the question which hung in the air...

"So – what is it that you have to do, to avoid that rather dreadful fate?"

"Marry. Marry within a year after my mourning ends, and marry a woman who is the daughter of an Earl or higher ranked nobleman."

Despite himself, Simon gave a burst of laughter.

"That doesn't seem such a terrible fate, Tarynholt – after all, we've all got to marry eventually!"

"True – but it's the two limitations – the year, and the status of the woman. Have you seen the 'eligible young women' who are left unmarried after last Season? And the ones due to come out next year, when I'll be out of mourning? There are very few of the right status, and those that do exist are..."

Robert stopped, shuddering, and took a very large gulp from his tankard.

"I see what you mean. But surely, there will be hope? Surely there is one you've not seen or heard about?"

"Not that I know of. But rest assured, I'll spend the rest of my mourning year assiduously studying Debrett's."

The other two nodded, and finished their ale.

Simon rose, and voiced what they all knew to be true.

"We'd best not slow you down then. It's not far to each of our estates from here, so we should be on our way. We'll just have to believe that someone will magically appear to save you from certain doom."

Chapter One

January 1819

Hannah Browning pulled her heavy coat around her, shivering in the cold wind, as the tears froze to her cheeks. In front of her, Mr Potter, the Lower Nettlefold Gravedigger, shovelled the last of the earth back into her father's grave, burying his body forever. The vicar from Upper Nettlefold, who had come to do the last rites for her father, patted her hand as he passed her.

"I must away back to my own church, Miss. Your father was a good man, and will be missed by all. I am sure that a new vicar will be appointed soon – but in the interim, if you need my help, just send a message."

Hannah nodded, and lifted a hand to brush away her tears.

"I will, thank you."

The vicar left, and Hannah stood there, as the villagers all slowly walked away, some with a kind word for her, others simply with a morose look. Once they were all gone, Mrs Bell came to her, and gently slipped an arm around her.

"Come Hannah, it's time we went home."

Hannah went, grateful for the woman beside her. Mrs Bell had been with her since she was a babe in arms, and had, even when she married, still remained as housekeeper for the vicarage. For the last five years she had spent all her time there, as her own husband had died an untimely death, carried off by an unexpected illness one winter.

Together, they crossed the graveyard, went past the church in which her father would never preach again, and along the path to the small house where Hannah had spent almost her whole life. It was supposed to be a verger's house – but this parish had not had a verger since before her father's time, and so he had chosen to live in the smaller house, close to his beloved church, and had dedicated the far larger house which was intended as the vicarage to more charitable use as an orphanage.

When the door shut behind them, and Mrs Bell hurried to build up the fire in the hearth, Hannah simply stood for a moment, as the shock of the lack of her father's presence struck her again. Then, with a sigh, she shook herself out of her melancholy, shrugged out of the coat, and hung it on the hooks near the door. There was nothing for it but to go on, to maintain the house and the church, and to do what she could to work out a way forward which would keep her, Mrs Bell, and the orphans, fed.

✷✷✷✷✷

Early February 1819

Mrs Bell bustled back into the small house by the church, her basket full of food from the small store in the village, and cheerfully settled the basket onto the kitchen table.

"Hannah! There's a letter for you."

Hannah came out of the study, a frown on her face.

"A letter? Who would be sending me a letter?"

"Well… I'm not certain – especially as it's only addressed to 'the late Vicar Browning's family'."

Hannah's heart sank. This could, she thought, be only one thing. She had known that, once her father was gone, it was only a matter of time until a new vicar would be appointed. The living for Lower Nettlefold was the new Earl of Dunsmore's to grant, and she had to hope that he had chosen a good man. She dropped into a chair at the table and broke the seal on the letter, as Mrs Bell emptied the basket and stored the food in the pantry.

To Mr Browning's family –

This letter serves to inform you that Mr Josiah Harris has been granted the living at Lower Nettlefold, and will be arriving to take up the position of Vicar at St. Stephens church at the end of March. Please ensure that the vicarage manor and the verger's house are vacated and ready for his occupation by that time.

Mr Harris is married, with seven children, so please ensure that the vicarage house is adequately prepared. I will inform you, closer to the time, of the exact date of Mr Harris' arrival, so that you can arrange for someone to be on hand to pass the keys and relevant information to Mr Harris.

Regards

Cholmondley and Sons

Solicitors to the Earl of Dunsmore.

Mrs Bell put on the kettle, and settled onto another chair at the table.

"You look pale, Hannah. Is there a problem?" Wordlessly, Hannah passed the letter to Mrs Bell, who read it carefully, and paled a little herself. "Only a month or so? That's… difficult… and with so many children – he will want the bigger house – where will the orphans go?"

"I don't know yet – but I will think of a solution – I must."

"And Hannah – where will you go? I still have my little cottage that Mr Bell left me, but you have nothing but the small amount of money your father left you, and your mother's jewellery."

"I... I don't know. I have an idea, but I will need to send some letters, urgently."

"Never fear then, if your idea doesn't work out, you are welcome in my cottage with me. It's very small, but at least no one could evict us from it..."

Hannah rose, and hurried around the table to hug Mrs Bell.

"Thank you! That lifts at least part of the weight from my heart. But still, the orphans, and Mrs Willis – where we might find for them to live worries me more! I will go and write some letters, immediately, in the hope that I can find a solution in time."

✱✱✱✱✱

Late February 1819

Hannah used her hip to push open the kitchen door, stepping inside and greeting Mrs Bell with a tired smile.

"I'm back."

"I can see that Hannah dear. I've just about got supper ready. It's not much, but it will fill your stomach." Mrs Bell continued stirring the soup, grateful for the chunks of potato and carrots which would provide the bone-weary Hannah some much needed nourishment. "Why don't you sit down and rest your feet for a wee bit?"

Hannah nodded her head and sighed.

"Thank you, I might do just that. The children were rather out of sorts today. This incessant rain has kept them inside for the better part of a week now and they are anxious to get outdoors again. I look forward to the springtime."

The children she spoke about were the wards of the orphanage. The dozen children had all come to the orphanage by different paths, and from different backgrounds, but they all shared one trait - they lacked parents, and any other relatives who might have cared for them.

Being the only daughter of the vicar, Hannah had always felt that it was her duty to try to bring some kind of happiness to their lives, even if it was nothing more than a paltry puppet show with hand puppets which she and Mrs Bell had fashioned from cast-off clothing. Her father had passed away two months ago now, but Hannah had continued to visit the elderly and the sick in the town, and to teach the children at the orphanage their lessons, and carry on as he would have wished.

Her father had been a gentle man whose compassion and wisdom had been sorely missed in Lower Nettlefold, where he'd served for more than twenty years. He'd done his best for the people of the village, and caring for the orphans had been a large part of that. After Hannah's mother had passed away seven years ago, when Hannah was just fourteen years old, she had taken on her mother's previous duties in helping to care for the children who lived in the orphanage, and was still doing so today.

Since her father's death, and receiving notice that a new Vicar would be arriving soon, Hannah had been corresponding with her mother's cousin – a woman she had never met, and who, until their first exchange of letters, had not even known of Hannah's existence. Now, that correspondence had borne fruit – at least in so much that Hannah had a possible way forward for her own life, and for her ability to continue to support the orphaned children.

"The rain will stop soon enough and then we'll be praying for it to start again. 'Tis the way it is."

Hannah smiled, feeling blessed to have the older woman's companionship.

"That's true."

Hannah went into the small parlour, and sank down into the chair near the hearth - it had been nearly two months since her father died, and the house still felt empty without his presence. The small house they had used as the vicarage only contained a parlour, a tiny study, a loft, and a single bedroom. Her father had used the loft as sleeping quarters, and the tiny study to write his sermons and maintain records, but his books had spilled out into the rest of th house. Hannah tilted her head back, and sadness filled her as she surveyed the bookshelves which lined the parlour walls.

Her father had been her best friend, and she missed him terribly. He'd been the victim of a highwayman on his way back from visiting a tiny outlying village. His death hadn't been discovered until the following morning and the entire district had mourned his passing.

Hannah closed her eyes and tried to focus on the changes which were coming to her life. Three weeks had gone by since the letter had arrived, informing her that the new vicar and his family would be arriving at the end of March. And she still had no certainty of alternative lodging, beyond Mrs Bell's kind offer. The problem with everything, of course, was that she had limited funds. And so she had written to her mother's cousin, and made a decision which would irrevocably change her life.

Mrs Bell approached her with a bowl of soup and a crust of bread.

"Here you are, dear. You just sit there and relax while you eat."

Hannah took the offering.

"Will you join me?"

"I'd be delighted to."

Mrs Bell retrieved a bowl of soup for herself and took a seat opposite Hannah. The fire crackled gently in the grate as they ate in silence for a while, each lost in their own thoughts. Eventually, Mrs Bell asked the question Hannah had known was coming.

"Did you post the letter?"

Hannah nodded.

"Yes. It should reach London sometime tomorrow. I was lucky – the Earl is going to London, leaving in the morning, and James Dobbins is the footman chosen to travel with his carriage this time. James promised that he would deliver it, in person, to Lady Deerwood, as she lives not far from the Earl's town house. So, by this time tomorrow, Lady Deerwood will know that I've accepted her kind invitation to come and stay with her. I only wish I knew how she will react when she sees me. She mentioned wanting to introduce me to society. I'm not sure how I feel about that."

"How she will react? I'm sure that she'll take to you, Hannah. You do look so like your mother, and they were best friends when they were children, not simply relatives."

Hannah sighed, trying to imagine her mother's youth, and rather failing.

"How can you be sure that she'll like me? After all, she didn't even know that I existed until a few weeks ago..."

"You'll be an instant success if she does introduce you to society, I'm sure. Remember - you are Lady Hannah – a title you are entitled to be known by, no matter how humbly you have gone about your life here. You are the granddaughter of an Earl, and the daughter of a nobleman, after all."

Hannah's mother's father was Francis Debenham, the Earl of Scartmoor. And Hannah's father had been her mother's first husband, and of the nobility, although she knew almost nothing of him. She knew that Charles Browning was not, in fact, her birth father – but until now, such things had never seemed to matter. Hannah had been happy living a simple life as a vicar's daughter, surrounded by the love of her mother and the man who she had always thought of as her father.

Now, she had to face the fact that she was entitled to be treated very differently, entitled to be seen in society, yet she knew nothing whatsoever about how to go on in such circumstances. She prayed that Lady Deerwood would understand the difficulties she faced.

Mrs Bell smiled as she reached across the table to pat Hannah's hand.

Hannah gave her a rueful grin.

"Perhaps – I might manage to be a success – or more likely, an embarrassment which forces Lady Deerwood's entire family to hide away in the country."

Mrs Bell shook her head.

"Never!"

"Thank you for your confidence in me, but I remember the few stories my mother told me about her days as a young girl entering society. It truly does not sound like a place I want to be. I've no wish to attend dances for the sole purpose of snaring a husband."

"You may enjoy having someone take care of you for a change. You take on too much."

"If I do not, who will? I will continue to do what I can, and pray that the new vicar will be so inclined. I know my father would never have wanted me to abandon the children."

"You are a good daughter and a compassionate young lady. Those children are lucky to have you on their side. If things don't work out in London... well, I've told you before, you are more than welcome to come and live with me. Until you work out what comes next."

Hannah smiled at the woman.

"Mrs Bell, I appreciate your kindness and friendship more than you can possibly imagine, but it is time for me to meet my only remaining relatives. My cousin has graciously invited me to stay with her in London, and I am hoping that, after a suitable period of getting to know one another, she might be inclined to pen me a reference. With a reference from someone of her stature, I will look for a governess position. That will hopefully provide me enough money that I will be able to send some to you, to help keep the orphans – wherever they must live, after the new vicar arrives."

"Oh Hannah, your parents would not want that for you," Mrs Bell said. "You are so accomplished and could do anything you set your mind to."

Hannah had been taught a variety of subjects normally reserved for males, her father having only one child and a wealth of knowledge to impart. Of course, she'd been taught, by her dearly beloved mother, to play the pianoforte, to paint with watercolours, and to stitch a straight seam. In addition, her father had taught her numbers, history, a love of literature, and philosophy. A little science had been thrown in from time to time, as well as a variety of languages. Hannah had proven, at a very early age, to be adept at learning things. Had she been born a male, she might have been sent to Eton, and then gone to Oxford. Instead, she'd been raised a vicar's daughter. For of course, women were not granted the opportunities that men were.

Hannah gave the housekeeper a sad smile.

"I know, but I really don't have any other options. Even after I sell what little jewellery my mother left me, I would barely be able to survive a month in town."

If that. Living in town is very expensive.

Or so she'd been told. She'd never been to London and was looking at her upcoming journey as a Grand Adventure.

Mrs Bell frowned.

"Surely there must be something else you can do?"

Hannah shook her head.

"I shall be very well. Tomorrow, I will sort through father's books and take out the ones I wish to keep. The bookseller from Upper Nettlefold will be arriving after lunch to take the rest."

"I will miss you, Hannah," Mrs Bell said, her eyes moist with unshed tears.

"And I will miss you as well. I promise to write often."

Hannah broke off as tears clogged her throat. She'd never known anything other than the village where she'd been raised. She was actually terrified of the changes which were about to occur in her life, but she was also determined to try to connect with her late mother's family.

If possible, she even hoped to meet her elusive grandfather – the man who had, for reasons she did not entirely understand for her mother had never spoken of the detail, cast off her mother, utterly.

This was her future and no matter how frightening it seemed, she was going to move forward. The orphans depended on her, after all.

Chapter Two

London Early March 1819

Robert watched the crowded ballroom with a cynical eye and a firmness to his lips that those who knew him well would be able to interpret. He was finding the evening deathly dull - not just marginally so, he was completely past feeling any interest in London and everything that went with it.

A fortnight earlier he'd been summoned to London to take his rightful place in the House of Lords, for the parliamentary session. His father, whose death, nearly two years ago, had left Robert not only with the title, but with that utterly obnoxious clause in his will, would no doubt have been delighted to see Robert here, considering the young ladies of the *ton*. For a moment, bitterness filled him – the year that clause had given him to marry a suitable woman, once he was out of mourning, was rapidly approaching its end, and he had yet to find a young lady of the correct status who did not make him turn away in horror.

Not that Robert actually wanted any of the social niceties he was forced to deal with. He'd been pleasantly enjoying life at the estate left to him by his mother, until necessity had brought him to London.

His mother had lived at Nettlerush Banks for the last fifteen years of her life and Robert had spent a lot of that time staying with her - they had been united in wishing to avoid his father's company. Even once she was gone, Robert had, most especially during the Season, preferred staying at Nettlerush Banks, which was on the road to Bath, a day and a half from London in good weather – for that allowed him to avoid the marriage minded young women, as well as his father.

The endless Soirees and Balls, the expectations of a member of the *ton,* were more than he was prepared to deal with. He was considered, by the matrons of the *ton,* to be both the most elusive, and the most eligible bachelor this Season - there had been quite the flurry of gossip when he had arrived in town, given his intense avoidance of the Season in previous years.

So now, at the age of twenty-seven, he was doomed to be hounded until his unmarried status was corrected. And, as a result of that damnable clause in the Will, he had no choice but to be there, to allow that pursuit of him to happen.

He turned his gaze towards the group of young women who clustered together with their mothers, all eagerly trying to gain his attention from across the room. None of them appealed at all.

Blast my father's eternal need to control everything!

His father had been furious when Robert had retired to the country, only coming to town once or twice a year, and choosing to spend the rest of his time on his friends' estates or with his mother. His father had seen that as a deliberate defection, which it was, and rather than allowing Robert to live his life in peace, he'd done everything possible to try to lure his son back into his control.

He hadn't succeeded in life, but in his death, he'd done a remarkable job. The threat of seeing all of his wealth and unencumbered properties go to his snivelling cousin, Herbert Calthorpe, was a strong enough motivator, where nothing else ever had been. Without the money and income-producing properties his father had held, Robert would be hard pressed to finance the entailed properties, and to support himself, and his tenants. He would end up a titled pauper while his witless cousin squandered everything!

His cousin hadn't the common sense given a goat, and cared only for the latest fashions and being seen at the right events. That and his many mistresses. Herbert had inherited a substantial sum of money from his mother, and if rumours were correct, he would be nearing financial ruin before this Season was complete. His stepfather was a Baron, but would leave his title to his own son. There was no money backing that title anyway, the Baron having married Herbert's mother for her wealth, which had now been nearly exhausted, by both men.

Robert could not allow it – so here he was doing what his father had wanted him to do, for so long. For he couldn't stand the thought of the imbecile frittering it all away on indulgences, destroying the ancestral Tarynholt properties, or the many other holdings his father had added to the family wealth in his lifetime. Hundreds of lives were at stake in the form of the tenants who worked the fields and farms, not to mention the household staff who would be put out onto the street were Herbert to be given a chance to ruin things.

Therefore, to meet the terms of his father's will, he needed a bride. And not just any bride. He needed a bride who at least equalled him in status – a bride who was the daughter of an Earl, a Marquess, or a Duke. His father had no doubt been afraid that Robert would use a common doxy, with the promise of a large purse for her troubles, to meet the terms of the Will. At least his father had respected Robert's intelligence enough to realise that he would try to escape the strictures of the Will. It was another source of bitterness that his father had never once shown him that much respect in life.

So the cunning old man had stipulated that Robert must marry within a year of the end of his mourning, and to a member of the *ton* who was equal to or higher ranked than Robert. Thus, his father had efficiently found a way to control his son for two years – for he had spent the year of mourning trying to find a way out of the requirement, and now the better part of the last year trying to identify a woman who met the conditions, and was also a person he might be able to stand to live with.

So far he had failed, and a bare three months remained before the deadline.

Sighing, he returned his attention to the occupants of the ballroom. Quickly cataloguing the young women present at tonight's event, he realised that not one of them was of high enough birth to qualify. There were several daughters of Barons and Viscounts who were unaware of his restrictions and had, in the short time that he had been in London so far, stopped at nothing to gain his attention. But the selection of eligible females this Season, who also met his father's status requirements, was very limited – there were only two young ladies, both of whom had already been spoken for by classmates of his from Eton.

The arrival of a new young lady caught his attention and he mentally cringed as he surveyed the newcomer. She was dressed dreadfully, in a mustard yellow gown which did nothing to conceal her rather large size. She laughed at something, shockingly loudly, and Robert grimaced at the harsh piercing sound as it echoed around the room.

"Who is that?"

His closest friend, Simon Hart, the Marquess of Marlby, looked in the direction of Robert's gaze, and tendered him a rather wry smile.

"That, my friend, is your only eligible option for a bride this Season. Lady Marigold Withershaw."

Simon was fully aware of Robert' father's Will and, while he had, since first being told of it, teased his friend mercilessly about his dilemma, the idea of Robert being stuck with Lady Marigold was even too frightening for him to contemplate.

Robert watched the rather portly lady strut around the ballroom, her bearing and demeanour as outlandish as her attire, her hideous laughter drowning out even the music.

"Marigold! And she has chosen to wear a gown of that colour? If that is an indication of her... taste... I shudder to think about what other things she might consider acceptable. There is absolutely no possibility that I am going to marry her!"

Simon chuckled.

"I can't say I blame you, but with only three months left to find a bride, you are quickly running out of choices."

Robert turned to his friend and gave him a determined look.

"I will not marry Lady Marigold. Yet somehow, I will be married by the end of May, because Cousin Herbert is not getting his hands on my properties. Or my father's money."

"Spoken like a true aristocrat."

Simon slapped him good-naturedly on the shoulder as another piercing shriek of unmannerly laughter cut through the music, and they both grimaced.

"An aristocrat with few options," said a soft voice behind him.

Robert turned just as an elegant woman reached her hand out to stop his retreat. Kitty Debenham, Marchioness of Haleston, was one of the *ton's* most influential women. Her husband, the Marquess of Haleston, was elderly, reclusive, and never attended these events. His much younger second wife, however, never missed an opportunity to do so. She was in her mid-thirties and had taken the *ton* by storm, arriving out of nowhere, ten years earlier. As a woman with significant standing in society, she did and said what she wanted, ignoring the whispers which went around behind her back about her husband, with no one being completely sure which of those rumours were true or not.

"Lady Haleston," Robert inclined his head in greeting. "You seem to find my... er, shall we say... predicament, of some amusement? I am all ears to your opinion."

Lady Haleston slipped her arm through his.

"Walk with me, Tarynholt. I may have a solution to what you refer to as your 'predicament'." The familiar action was likely to draw raised brows from the dowagers who had nothing better to do than cast aspersions on the younger members of the *ton*, but given Lady Haleston's status, they would keep their opinions to themselves. She looked at Simon and waved him off, "Your presence is not needed for this conversation, Marlby."

Robert inclined his head and motioned for his friend to give them some privacy.

"I'll catch up with you later at the club."

"Very good."

Lord Marlby bowed to Lady Haleston, turned on his heel and strolled across the room in search of his next dance partner.

Robert turned his attention back to the lady on his arm.

"So, do tell. Do you know of another eligible young lady, whom I might consider marrying, who meets the terms of my father's Will?"

Lady Haleston smiled.

"As a matter of fact, I do. Join me in the gardens and I will tell you a story."

Robert led her out of the stuffy ballroom, and they settled on a bench – still in full view of people on the terrace, but far enough away to prevent eavesdropping. He listened with interest as she told a story about love and the consequences which had followed.

✳✳✳✳✳

Lower Nettlefold, March 1819

Hannah tried not to cry as the bookseller packed up the last of her father's books. She'd kept only a few of her favourites, and several of the study tomes he had written copious notes in. The rest had been sold for mere pennies, but the sum was enough to ensure that she would be able to travel to London by stage coach.

The journey to London, on the coach which she could afford, would take two days, although a lighter private carriage could do it in one, she had been told.

The Innkeeper had promised to keep a ticket for her, for two days from now, and she would pay for that once she had packed everything – not that she had very much to pack. She turned her attention to finishing the task of sorting through her belongings.

"Mrs Bell?" she called out, needing help to lift the valise containing the books she had kept down to the floor. "Mrs Bell?"

When no answer was received, Hannah dusted her hands off on her apron and climbed down the ladder, looking around for the woman. She stepped into the kitchen, but did not see Mrs Bell. Then, the distant sound of an arriving carriage captured her attention. Now that her father was gone, no one called on them, so why would a carriage be coming down the lane to the church?

"What now?"

She went to the front door and pulled it open, intending to look out to see who it was. But she was caught off guard when the sight of a black leather encased fist, raised and ready to knock on the door, greeted her. She jumped and stepped back with a small squeak of alarm, watching as the gloved hand dropped down to the side of the most handsome man she had ever laid eyes on.

"I beg your pardon," his deep voice washed over her as he bowed slightly at the waist. "I am seeking Lady Hannah Charteris."

That name - the one she had been told was hers, but which she had never, in her life, used. How did he know that name, and to find her here? She wasn't ready to be that person – although she supposed that in London….

She blinked at him and then, clearing her throat, found her voice.

"It's just Hannah."

She stood mesmerised as she scanned him from head to toe then, as she did, became aware of the inappropriateness of her gaze. It was several long moments of silence and a knowing smile upon his lips which brought her attention to the fact that she had been gawking at him like a smitten green girl who had never seen a man before.

When his own eyes took a similar inventory of her, she couldn't contain the blush which rose to her cheeks. She straightened her spine.

"How may I assist you?"

The gentleman's eyes travelled back up to her own and then he offered her another slight bow.

"Robert Calthorpe, Lord Tarynholt, at your service."

Wondering why a Lord was standing on the front step of the vicarage, Hannah asked.

"Lord Tarynholt. Are you lost?"

He straightened.

"No, my Lady." His lips curled into a devastating smile, and she felt as if she might melt from the heat of his gaze. "Lady Deerwood bid me to collect you and see that you are brought safely to her in London."

"Lady Deerwood sent you?"

Hannah was surprised that her mother's cousin would send a man to escort her all the way to London – especially a man such as this!

She stepped forward, relieved when she saw a handsome carriage, complete with a coachman and a footman, waiting. From inside the carriage, a girl in a maid's cap peeked out. A shiny black stallion pawed the ground beside the carriage and a groom struggled to hold onto the reins of the impatient horse while his rider spoke to Hannah.

The sound of the man's voice brought her eyes back to his own.

"Your cousin was unable to make the journey herself, but she asked if I would escort you to her home. Since I fancied some fresh air and was happy to escape the city, I was pleased to agree to her request. I have brought a comfortable carriage, and a maid to attend you."

Hannah was stunned into speechlessness. Only the arrival of Mrs Bell nudged her from her silence and into stammering speech.

"Mrs Bell, this is Lord Tarynholt. He has come to escort me to London."

"Oh my! Well, don't keep him standing in the doorway – do show him into the parlour. I'll see about making some tea, and I think there are some scones left from breakfast."

The older woman scurried to the sideboard and started gathering cups, saucers, and plates.

"Mrs Bell, do not put yourself out on my account. I simply wanted to make Lady Hannah's acquaintance and to inquire at what time tomorrow she would be ready to travel."

Lord Tarynholt remained at the doorway and made no attempt to enter the cottage. Hannah raised an eyebrow.

"Tomorrow? I had not planned to travel until the day after." After a moment's silence, she stated more firmly, "I simply cannot leave tomorrow."

Lord Tarynholt paused, and Hannah suspected that he was trying not to display impatience at the impertinence of her statement, but she would not be moved on this. Perhaps her manners were not those of high society, but if she did not stand up for herself from the start, all would be lost. After a moment, he appeared to swallow his annoyance.

"May I know why? Is there a problem which I can help you attend to? I assure you, whatever is needed to help you complete your preparations can be easily dealt with."

Hannah shook her head.

"No. And it is not a problem, but an obligation." The children at the orphanage had planned a small going away party for her, to take place the following afternoon, and Hannah wouldn't disappoint them. "I appreciate my cousin's kindness, but I simply cannot travel until the day after next. If the delay interferes with your schedule, I will continue with my original plans and travel on the stage coach. Now, I believe Mrs Bell mentioned tea."

She stepped back and gestured with her hand for him to enter the small house.

Lord Tarynholt shook his head.

"No, that would not be appropriate. Single young ladies do not travel by stage coach unescorted. I will return the day after tomorrow at first light to collect you, and whatever belongings you wish to take with you. Please be ready, as we have a long way to go." He offered her a bow, and then nodded to Mrs Bell, who still lingered behind her. "Good day."

Hannah watched him mount the massive stallion, and ride off up the lane, followed by his carriage. He was an impressive figure atop the black horse, and she watched him until he disappeared from her sight. The thought of travelling with him, even if not in close proximity, made her feel rather overheated. She had never considered such a thing in her life – but… it was not without appeal. She shut the door then and turned to Mrs Bell.

"Why do you think my cousin sent such a man to be my escort?"

Mrs Bell smiled at her and gave her a conspiratorial wink.

"I don't think that it matters why he has come – you can ask your cousin that question when you get to London. Whatever her reasons, he is remarkably handsome. Maybe you won't have to worry about getting that reference after all. Perhaps you'll be getting a husband instead."

Hannah stared at Mrs Bell, a little shocked by her words, then laughed.

"A husband? Surely not. I'm sure he is just a friend doing another friend a favour."

Mrs Bell smiled indulgently.

"Believe what you will. Time will tell. I'll get that tea for us. You should go and finish packing. We have a full day with the children tomorrow and I do believe that gentleman truly means to be here before the sun rises the day after. You wouldn't want to keep a man like that waiting."

Mrs Bell giggled to herself as she set about making tea and Hannah shook her head at the foolish notion in her companion's head. Although… if she was to have a husband, she could not deny the fact that she would prefer a man who looked attractive…

30

She finished packing the books she had decided to keep, along with her few clothes, her mind drifting often to the imposing man who would come to take her to London. She had never before met a man such as he, and she only hoped that all of the fine young men in London did not look like him. Otherwise, she'd have a hard time concentrating on anything else but finding the husband Mrs Bell seemed to think she required.

Hannah wasn't opposed to the idea of marrying, but if she was going to marry, she wanted a marriage based on love, like the marriage her parents had enjoyed. She was a romantic, and not willing to settle for anything less. Although she certainly hoped her future husband would also be as handsome as Lord Tarynholt.

She felt her cheeks become warm as she pondered that thought.

She would marry for love, or not at all.

"I am so nervous, Kitty dear. What will she be like? Will she look like her mother? To think that, for all these years, I never knew that she existed!"

Annabelle Melling, Countess of Deerwood, forced herself to lift her tea cup and sip, but the nervous energy which filled her did not dissipate. Opposite her, the Marchioness of Haleston smiled reassuringly.

"Annabelle, I am sure that everything will go wonderfully. It does not matter that she was raised by a country Vicar – her father was a Duke, and I am sure that her mother taught her at least a modicum of good society behaviour, before she died. Indeed, being raised by a Vicar will likely have made her kinder and far less duplicitous than most of the ton!"

Annabelle laughed at that, for Kitty was right.

"Do you think we can hope that they will like each other?"

"We can certainly hope. But surely, if an Earl expresses interest in her, she is unlikely to hesitate – for that would give her a far better quality of life than she will have had as a vicar's daughter? I can personally attest to just how much difference status makes."

"Perhaps – but she is Eleanor's daughter, and Eleanor was stubborn, and went her own way – which is why Hannah has been raised where she has. It is entirely likely that Hannah takes after her mother…"

"Then, Annabelle dear, we shall just have to make sure that they have ample opportunity to see each other, and pray that there will be a natural attraction…"

Chapter Three

"Hannah! Hannah!"

The sound of children chanting her name caused Hannah to smile in delight - a mistake, since she was currently trying to keep from falling down after spinning herself around the requisite ten times.

The children were always thinking up new games to play, as well as inventing new variations on old games, and tag was one of their favourites. They'd come up with a clever way to even out the odds, whenever the older children or adults were playing with them. They had to spin around ten times before attempting to catch the younger players.

Hannah stopped spinning, laughing as the world spun around her crazily. She could see the children taunting her, managing to keep just out of her reach, and she staggered towards them, her hands outstretched as she attempted to tag one of them.

Mrs Willis, the widow tasked with watching over the orphans, stood nearby, an indulgent smile upon her face. When Jimmy, a precocious child who'd recently become a resident of the orphanage, stepped up behind Hannah and poked her with the stick in his hand, Mrs Willis' smile faded away and she scolded him sternly.

"Jimmy! That is inappropriate. You may sit out the rest of this game."

The sound of her stern voice and the sight of Jimmy's crestfallen face stole the fun from the game for Hannah and she stopped chasing the children and quietly called a halt to the game. She looked at the little faces she was going to sorely miss, and sent them to see Mrs Bell - she and the housekeeper had stayed up late the night before making honey cakes for the children, one of their favourite treats.

Jimmy had joined Mrs Willis, and Hannah walked towards them. She ignored the sound of horses in the distance, as she concentrated on the little boy who was obviously fighting back tears.

"I'm sorry, Mrs Willis. I didn't mean to hurt her."

"That is not the point, Jimmy. Young men do not poke others with sticks!"

"Mrs Willis, I don't believe that Jimmy meant me any harm. May I speak with him?"

Mrs Willis smiled and nodded her head.

"Of course, Miss. I'll just go and help Mrs Bell serve the treats."

Hannah waited until the older woman had moved away before she squatted down so that she and Jimmy were eye-level with one another.

"Jimmy?"

His bottom lip quivered and then he launched himself into her arms, sending her sprawling backwards into the dirt in a flurry of skirts and dust.

"Now there!" a masculine voice called out from behind her.

Hannah tried to turn her head, but Jimmy had wrapped his little arms around her neck. She was still trying to untangle their limbs when Jimmy's weight was suddenly lifted from her, amidst his cry of fright.

"Don't hurt me, sir. Please, don't hurt me. I didn't mean to knock her over."

"Hush!"

34

Hannah had managed to straighten out her skirts and now looked up from the dirt to see Lord Tarynholt holding a very scared looking Jimmy by the back of his shirt, his feet dangling off the ground.

She scrambled to her feet.

"Put that child down! What do you mean coming here and accosting him?"

"Me, accosting him? I rather think it is he who has been doing the accosting – I saw him knock you over."

Lord Tarynholt sounded incredulous. Hannah reached out and tried to pull Jimmy from his hands.

"Let him go!"

*****

Robert stepped forward, retaining his hold on the child, and bringing himself within inches of the very alluring young lady who seemed to care not that her skirts were covered in dust, or that her hair pins were beginning to come loose – which somehow, only made her the more intriguing.

When Jimmy tried to kick at him, accidentally kicking Hannah instead, Robert had reached the end of his patience. He hauled the child up and quietly told him.

"Apologise. Now."

Jimmy gulped and turned to look at Hannah over his shoulder.

"I'm sorry, Miss."

Robert could hear the sincerity in the child's voice, and released him into Hannah's grasp. She really was not at all like he had expected, when Lady Deerwood had suggested that he come and escort her to London, as a way to see if she might be a solution to his problem. Certainly, nothing he had seen so far bore any resemblance to the ladies of the *ton* that he was used to.

✱✱✱✱✱

Hannah finally managed to pull Jimmy away from Lord Tarynholt, and hugged the young boy close for a moment.

"It was an accident, Jimmy, I know that you didn't mean to knock me over. I'm all right, but please do me a favour?"

Jimmy bobbed his head in an acquiescent nod, his wide blue eyes watching her in admiration and no small measure of infatuation.

She smiled at him.

"Let's leave the sticks on the ground where they belong. If one of the little ones decided to play with those sticks, someone could become seriously hurt."

Jimmy nodded his head.

"I won't let them play with sticks. I'll make sure they don't."

"Thank you. Now, I believe that Mrs Bell is keeping some honey cakes just for you."

Jimmy's eyes lit up and he launched himself at her waist once again, but this time she was ready for him. She absorbed the impact from his body, returning his hug even as tears stung her eyes. She was going to miss all of the children, but Jimmy most especially.

He had come to the orphanage half-starved and filthy. As far as everyone could determine, the child had not had a proper bath in months, or perhaps years, and convincing him that the water meant him no harm had been quite a feat. Hannah had finally intervened, taking him by the hand and marching him down to the nearby stream. She'd then surprised them all by walking right into the water with him. His first bath had commenced with his clothes on, and their lips turning blue from the chilliness of the water. He'd quickly realised that taking a bath indoors and with water heated over the coals was a much better experience.

36

As Jimmy released her and set off to claim his honey cakes, Hannah watched the children for another minute before turning her attention to Lord Tarynholt and the other gentleman who had ridden into the meadow with him, who now stood a little back from them, holding both horses.

She remembered her manners and inclined her head.

"My Lord, may I inquire why you are here today? I thought we were traveling to London tomorrow."

Lord Tarynholt raised a brow.

"It would seem that I am here for the purpose of rescuing you from the clutches of overexuberant children." He ended his statement with a smile and then turned to watch the children, "Where are their parents?"

"They have no parents. Those children are residents of the orphanage."

And I'm going to miss them so much when I leave here.

Part of her reason for traveling to London was to obtain a good position somewhere, in the hope that she would be able to earn enough that she might send funds back for the children's care. The vicarage had been funding the orphanage since Hannah could remember, but it wasn't required of the Vicar – it had been her father's personal charitable endeavour.

Mrs Willis had expressed her fears that the new vicar would not be so inclined. Hannah shared her fear, especially since the new vicar had not one, but seven children of his own, and she was still fretting about where the children might be moved to, when the new Vicar took possession of this manor. Somehow, she would find a solution – or Mrs Bell would, while she was away.

The sound of Lord Tarynholt clearing his throat pulled her thoughts back to the present, and she continued with the explanation she had been giving him. He was, she thought, remarkable patient, compared to most men she had met.

"Thank you for your assistance, but as you can see, it was unnecessary. I enjoy the children's energy and do not mind at all a little dust. Seeing them happy is more important than a clean dress."

✱✱✱✱✱

Robert was becoming more intrigued by the minute with this young woman who was not in the least cowed by his presence, nor seemingly interested in garnering his attentions.

"Who cares for these children?"

He counted an even dozen of them, ranging in ages from what he estimated to be three to ten.

"Mrs Willis is the house mother, and I have been teaching them their studies and making sure that there are adequate supplies. But now... I...," she paused, obviously concerned about something, but not willing to voice it. After a moment, she swallowed, and gave him a smile, "They will be well looked after. Was there something you required?"

Marlby stepped forward at that point and bowed to Hannah.

"I believe that Lord Tarynholt has forgotten his manners."

Robert gritted his teeth, but made the requisite introduction.

"May I introduce Simon Hart, the Marquess of Marlby. Simon, this is Lady Hannah Charteris."

As Robert watched, Hannah smiled at Simon, seeming a little unsure, a faint blush staining her cheeks when he took the hand she offered him and kissed the back of her glove. Robert rolled his eyes as Simon released her hand, chuckling softly. Hannah, thankfully, seemed unaware of the hidden messages which were silently passing between the two men.

"I'm pleased to meet you."

"The pleasure is all mine, I assure you." Simon backed away when Robert sent him a further glare, "I'll leave you to discuss our travel arrangements."

Hannah watched him retreat before turning back to Robert.

"Travel arrangements? Is the Marquess traveling to London with us?"

"Yes." Robert answered her abruptly and without further explanation, her reaction to Simon's gallantry annoying him for some reason. "I thought that you had obligations to fulfil and packing to complete, preventing you from traveling today. Yet you have time to play games with these children?"

She cocked her head to the side, and for a moment he thought that she would reprimand him for the judgmental tone in his voice, but after a moment she appeared to choose to ignore it, and simply offered an explanation calmly.

"I am already packed. And the obligation was this party. The children planned it for me, as a farewell before I leave for London. It is important to them, particularly as I shall miss the Easter festivities this year." Robert considered her explanation, and found himself unable to voice any further complaint about her delaying their departure. "Would you care to join us?"

Robert watched her cheeks turn pinker as she issued the invitation and he found himself fascinated. He turned towards the children who had all gathered around Simon's and his horses and were taking turns stroking their noses and feeding them small pieces of their honey cakes.

"It would seem I have little choice."

He gestured with his hand for her to precede him and then followed her, watching the sway of her skirts, and liking what he saw. For the next hour or so, he watched her interact with the children.

He was amazed to see how easily, and enthusiastically, she handled their questions.

The children soiled her skirts with their hands, yet she seemed utterly unconcerned, and he noticed that the younger children had no qualms about coaxing her to lift them up. She did so with a smile, and even when two of the older boys started arguing, she calmly dealt with it, hugging both boys after they apologised to one another.

She was an enigma and he found himself wondering how she would cope with the ballrooms of London. Lady Deerwood, her mother's cousin, had not even known of Lady Hannah's existence until several weeks earlier - Kitty, one of Lady Deerwood's closest friends, had been privy to the meek letter which Lady Hannah had written, requesting permission to visit her mother's cousin and possibly meet her grandfather, the Earl of Scartmoor.

Lady Eleanor, the only daughter of the Earl of Scartmoor, had wished to marry a commoner, and, when forbidden to do so by her father, had married the Duke he had chosen – a man far older than she was. But not two years after their marriage the Duke had died, and the Lady had simply run away, and gone to marry the man she had loved from the start. The Earl of Scartmoor had washed his hands of his daughter, and broken off all lines of communication, so that the Lady had simply disappeared from society completely, two decades ago now. What no one, other than the Earl, had known at the time was that Eleanor had borne a child to the Duke during their short marriage.

Lady Deerwood had been shocked to receive a letter from her cousin's daughter, informing her that both of her parents had passed away – for the girl obviously had regarded the Vicar who had raised her as her father - and requesting an opportunity to meet her other family members and try to rectify things with her grandfather. Her mother had told her at least the outline of the truth of it all when she was a child, but it had not seemed significant to her then, apparently.

Robert had listened with interest as Kitty, Lady Haleston, told him that the girl's plan was to meet her grandfather, and then to get a letter of reference in the hope of obtaining a governess position. The idea that the granddaughter of an Earl, the daughter of a Duke, would even consider doing such a thing was preposterous.

Lady Deerwood had invited Hannah to join her in London and then, at Kitty's prompting, began making her own arrangements for the girl's future. Kitty had told him that, not even knowing what Hannah looked like, nor her demeanour or manners, Kitty's head had begun to stir with the idea that Lady Hannah was the answer to Robert's need for a bride to meet the conditions of his father's Will.

When Kitty had shared this news with him, he'd agreed to travel to Lower Nettlefold and make the young lady's acquaintance, on the pretence of being her escort to London. He had, of course, also brought one of the maids from Lady Deerwood's household to attend Lady Hannah, for Lady Deerwood had quite rightly assumed that the girl would likely not have a maid of her own. By escorting her to London, he could get a look at her without her knowing anything of his reasons, and he could do so away from the prying eyes of the *ton*. There was enough gossip about him as it was, without him wishing to risk any more!

He had promised to give Lady Haleston an answer upon their arrival as to whether or not he thought the young lady a viable candidate for the position of his wife. After having met her yesterday, and watching her interact with both children and adults today, he couldn't wait to see how she handled the dragons of society. Her naiveté would be a breath of fresh air at the events which had become stale and lifeless in his eyes. And even if she caused rather a stir, he would be pleased to see some of the judgemental gossips disconcerted.

He suspected that Lady Hannah was going to take the *ton* by storm. He just wasn't quite sure if it would be a gentle misting, or a torrential downpour. Either way, he planned to have a front row seat and, at the end of the day, he planned to have her by his side. The thought came to him then that his father would have been scandalised by the concept, and apoplectic that Robert had managed to find a woman with no education in being a lady of the *ton,* yet who met all of the requirements stipulated.

Equally, he suspected that the gossips of the *ton* would be shocked – which prospect was pleasing to him, as well.

It was obvious that Lady Hannah knew nothing about how to be an Earl's wife, a Countess, but with Lady Haleston's promised support, and Lady Deerwood to give her instruction, she would learn all that was necessary. And, if he married her, as she was a Duke's daughter, he would fulfil the requirements of his father's Will and retain the properties and funds to maintain them, which should have been his rightful inheritance from the start.

As the afternoon wore on and the children's energy began to fade, for the first time in years, he found himself actually looking forward to being in town during the height of the Season. Two months from now, he would be a married man.

Now he just needed to convince the lady he'd set his sights on that he was a much better option than becoming a governess. A feat which shouldn't pose any significant problems, from his point of view.

Surely, he thought wryly, marrying him would seem a better prospect to her, than a life in service?

Chapter Four

Hannah nearly slid from the seat of the carriage for the fourth time, her frustration with the travel experience marring her normally pleasant disposition. She righted herself and then pulled out the walking stick she'd discovered beneath the bench on her first tumble to the carriage floor. She raised it and pounded it against the roof of the carriage in a desperate attempt to get the coachman to stop the conveyance. She just needed a few moments respite, or she was in serious danger of losing the contents of her stomach!

The maid on the other seat looked quite as uncomfortable as Hannah felt, but seemed afraid to express her discomfort. So, a short pause would do them both good.

She listened as the coachman called to the horses, bringing the carriage to a stop a few minutes later, once again causing Hannah to scramble to remain seated. Then, the door was opened by the scowling footman.

"Here now! What's the problem?"

"Sir, I believe that answering that particular question will only result in hurting your feelings, so I shall refrain from doing so. Could you please put the steps down so that I may step out?"

The footman did so, offering his hand as she gingerly stepped down.

Her relief at having her feet on solid ground, which wasn't lurching about, was immediate. From up on the box, the coachman called down to her.

"My Lady, the road is better just up ahead. After the recent rains, this section of the road is quite rutted and difficult – much more so than usual."

She gave the coachman a smile.

"I understand, but I still require a few moments before we continue. I am sure that you wouldn't want the cleaning task which would result if I, or Mary here, cast up my accounts whilst we were travelling."

The coachman and the footman both rather paled at the picture her words obviously raised in their minds.

"Right you are, my Lady – you take a few minutes then – just take care that you don't slip in the mud."

The footman helped her up to the verge, where rather limp grass remained, then inclined his head and stepped back to stand by the horses. She took a few hesitant steps, and once she was sure she had gained her equilibrium, she walked a short distance away, looking out between the trees at the rolling fields beyond.

Mary, the maid, followed her, as if she did not know what else to do. But as they went, she whispered, "Thank you, my Lady."

Hannah turned back to the two men who were impatiently waiting for her.

"Where are we?"

"About fifteen miles from the outskirts of London." Lord Marlby, who had just ridden up to where they were stopped, closely followed by Lord Tarynholt, answered her query. "If you're looking for the city, you'll need to look behind you."

Hannah nodded and then walked past the carriage, her eyes going wide as the open fields and trees seemed to become thinner. In the distance she could barely make out what looked like a sea of buildings, and she found herself anxiously wanting to see more.

"That's London?"

"Yes, my Lady. Are you ready to continue?"

The footman sounded hopeful.

Hannah was somewhat relieved that they would not be trying to find lodging for the night, as she would have been required to do had she gone with her original plan. When they had stopped for a midday meal, the Inn had been shocking to her. It was far larger than the small Inn in Lower Nettlefold. Horses, carriages, aristocracy, and servants had been milling around, with not enough room for anyone to fully relax, and a myriad of voices creating a very hectic scene.

She had eaten a crust of bread and some cheese, but the meat had not been properly cooked, and the room had been filled to overflowing with other travellers, even in the private parlour they kept for the upper classes.

Lord Tarynholt, to his credit, had found the situation untenable and requested that better food be prepared for them to take with them as they continued on their journey.

"Helmsly, shall we proceed?"

Lord Tarynholt brought his magnificent horse to a stop a short distance away. He looked her over carefully, before giving the carriage the same thorough glance.

"Yes, my Lord. That is, if... I trust that Lady Hannah is feeling better now?"

The coachman knew who his master was, but was nevertheless concerned about his female passenger. Lord Tarynholt turned his deep blue eyes onto her, dismounting from his horse and striding towards her.

Hannah felt her face heat under his scrutiny, and she backed away.

"I am ready to continue."

"Why did you ask the coachman to stop?" he asked, following her as she made her way to the steps of the carriage. "Are you ill?"

His inquiry was softly spoken, and there was a look of concern on his face.

"No, I was simply tired of being jostled around like a sack of potatoes. The coachman assures me that the road is more passable up ahead."

"It is. I'm sorry for your discomfort, I will instruct the coachman to maintain a slower pace."

"Please do not. That would only prolong our journey. I will do my best to not slow us down again." With that, she lifted her skirt and entered the carriage, arranging her skirts around her ankles and preparing for the rest of the journey. Mary followed her, and settled onto the other seat. Hannah turned her head to see Lord Tarynholt watching her, and offered him a pleasant smile. "I'm ready to go."

He gave her another look, and then closed the door. She heard him instruct the coachman to avoid the ruts as much as possible, and then a few minutes later, the carriage began moving again. Over the next three hours, the ride did become much smoother, and she was able to close her eyes and rest a bit. She drifted into half sleep, and the sounds of the carriage around her seemed to blur into the sounds of a ballroom – or at least what her mind imagined a ballroom to sound like. In the dream, Lord Tarynholt was beside her, and she was acutely conscious of the warmth of his arm beneath her hand.

The sun was beginning to set as the cry from the footman came up that they were entering London.

Hannah came awake, startled out of her dream just as they were about to dance a waltz, and after a moment of flushed confusion, she leaned towards the window of the carriage, her eyes wide as she got her first glimpse of the town. She was tired, dusty, and her body ached, and yet a strange excitement filled her.

This is my Grand Adventure.

*****

Mayfair March 1819

Hannah looked up at the grand house as she stepped down from the carriage and tried not to appear too out of place. She followed Lord Tarynholt to the door, amazed when it was opened, before he could even knock, by a uniformed butler. Lord Marlby had already left them, to go to his club.

"How did...?"

Lord Tarynholt smiled at her and she bit her lip, feeling completely out of her element. She shook her head, rather than finishing her question.

"Good evening, sir. Lady Deerwood will join you shortly."

"Very good, Milton. Is Lord Deerwood in this evening?"

"No, sir. I believe he is at his club."

"I will see him later then. Milton, this is Lady Hannah. Please ask Mrs Cummings if she could have a light supper sent to the parlour."

"Right away, sir. Welcome to London, my Lady."

Hannah nodded her head as she looked around her, taking in the elegant furnishings, the crystal chandelier, and the highly polished wood panelling. The house was breath-taking, and she realised that her mother's cousin had indeed married well.

"This way," the butler said, leading them down a short hallway to a point where he opened two doors and gestured for them to enter the parlour. On the far side of the room there were large windows, and closer, several couches were positioned in front of the oversized hearth, and a variety of historical pictures hung on the walls.

"Hannah, it's so good to finally meet you."

Hannah turned, to discover an elegant woman stepping through the doorway. She was dressed in a gold brocade gown, her hair beautifully coifed atop her head, and a warm smile upon her lips.

She glided across the room and took Hannah's hands in her own.

"You are the absolute image of your mother!"

Hannah allowed herself to be pulled in for a brief hug.

"Lady Deerwood?"

The woman smiled.

"Yes, but please do just call me Annabelle. We're family, after all."

Hannah immediately felt comfortable with the woman, far more so than she had expected.

"If you wish it, I would be honoured to do so."

When Annabelle then turned to Lord Tarynholt, Hannah watched as he bowed low over her hand and kissed the back of it.

"Thank you for escorting Lady Hannah to our home."

"It was my pleasure, my Lady. Now, I will leave you to get to know each other. I trust that Lady Haleston and yourself were successful in your plans?"

"Yes. The modiste will be here tomorrow morning early, and I've already obtained an invitation for Lady Hannah to attend Almack's this coming Wednesday. Will we see you there?"

Annabelle spoke politely but there was a twinkle in her eyes. Lord Tarynholt looked at Hannah as he answered.

"Most certainly." He then bowed over Annabelle's hand before turning his attention back to Hannah. "I hope you will save the first dance for me?"

"Dance?" Hannah asked, stunned.

"She would be delighted to do so. Now, as we have much to do in the next five days, I would like to get to know my cousin a little better."

"Ladies, I will see you five days from now."

Hannah blushed when he bowed low to her before striding from the room. She watched him until he was out of sight and then turned back to her hostess, to find Annabelle watching her with a smile.

"I'm so glad you have arrived safely, and hopefully no worse for wear. Now, come, sit and eat and tell me everything."

"Everything?"

Hannah's voice was a little uncertain as she spoke, wondering just what Annabelle might conceive to be included in 'everything'.

"Absolutely everything. I remember your mother from when we were young girls. I only wish I had enquired more deeply about her, sooner. Her father can be very difficult to deal with."

"My grandfather?"

"Yes. My uncle. I'm afraid he's not well."

Hannah nodded her head and then asked the question which was closest in her thoughts.

"Does he reside in London?"

"Yes, but he does not receive visitors. He is a bit eccentric and reclusive, and has chosen to keep to himself."

"But how am I to see him if he doesn't receive visitors?"

Hannah was filled with dismay, but Annabelle smiled at her.

"You leave that to me. Now, I've instructed the maids to heat water and take it upstairs to your rooms. I haven't travelled any great distance for a good while, but I remember how uncomfortable a carriage can be on rutted roads. The modiste will be here in the morning, and then we shall make a trip to Bond Street and procure everything else you might need for a proper Season."

"Oh no!" Hannah declared. "My Lady, Annabelle, you've misunderstood my reason for coming to you. I have no desire to partake in the social whirl."

"Nonsense! Every young lady looks forward to attending the Soirees and Balls which come with the Season. Being introduced at Almack's is the first step, and then the invitations will start flooding in."

"But I don't even know how to dance. And I'm sure that my attire is not anything near the standard which will be expected."

"That is why the modiste is coming tomorrow morning."

Annabelle smiled happily at her again, but Hannah felt her heart drop – how could she explain just how little money she had available?

"Please, I appreciate you arranging things, but even if I wanted to partake of the activities of the Season, I'm afraid that my funds are not sufficient."

"It is my pleasure to sponsor you. It will be good practice for the future, when my own daughter is ready to be presented to Society."

"You have children?"

Annabelle placed a hand on her stomach.

"My son is at Eton, but now, I hope for a daughter, after so many years without another child arriving. I am due in the autumn. George says we will leave town after Easter, when it should still be safe for me to travel, and retire to our country estate."

"Congratulations," Hannah told her. "But you must not tire yourself on my account. I truly only wrote to you because..."

"...you were hoping for a letter of reference," Annabelle finished Hannah's sentence for her. "I remember, dear. However, I believe we can do much better than that. After all, you are the granddaughter of an Earl, and the daughter of a Duke."

"What does that matter?" Then, worried that her question may appear rude, she added, "Forgive me, but I was not raised to be concerned with titles and do not understand how it should affect my ability to find a governess position."

Annabelle poured the tea which a maid had delivered, and Hannah carefully selected several small sandwiches, now acutely aware of how hungry she had become during the journey.

"This year, eligible young ladies are in short supply. I believe that we can find you a good husband by the time the Season ends, even though we are starting late."

Hannah's eyes widened.

"A husband? But, truly, I hadn't considered such a thing."

"You just leave all of that to me."

Annabelle seemed so sure that Hannah would want a husband, and Hannah had not expected her to make that assumption. She sat quietly, not wanting to seem ungrateful to her cousin, who was being so kind to her. But then little Jimmy's face came to mind, and she found herself shaking her head.

"I'm sorry, but I really need to find a position as a governess. There are children depending upon me."

"Children?!"

Annabelle looked completely shocked, and Hannah almost laughed, realising that a rapid explanation was in order.

"The orphans. My father started an orphanage, and the vicarage financed their upkeep, but now, the new vicar has seven children of his own and I fear he will no longer provide for them. Indeed, with such a large family of his own, he will want to live in the manor which they now occupy. I must find a paying position as soon as possible so that I can see to their welfare."

Annabelle looked at her, shaking her head.

"The orphans are surely not your responsibility."

Hannah felt tears sting her eyes.

"But they are. I promised I would find a way." She stopped and gathered control of her emotions, "I truly do appreciate your wishing to help me find a husband, but I have no dowry, and my requirements for a husband would make me even less desirable."

Annabelle raised a brow.

"Your requirements?"

Hannah gave her a tired nod.

"I will only marry for love - as my parents did. Nothing less. And now I would have to know that my husband was prepared to provide me the funds necessary to see that the orphans were well cared for. I doubt that is a desirable prospect for any gentleman."

Annabelle looked at her and then gave her a secretive smile.

"Why don't you let the young men of the *ton* decide that? Give me a month, and if you haven't found a man you can love, who will provide for the children of the orphanage, I will write you that letter of reference."

Hannah wrung her hands, feeling overwhelmed by the suggestion, and the hope that it provided, in a manner which she had not previously contemplated, but she still anguished over the delay. It would soon be Easter and she hoped to be placed in a governess position in the country, not far from Lower Nettlefold, before then. She and Mrs Bell had dreamed of dying eggs and surprising the children with an egg roll and sewing Easter bonnets for each of the girls, some of whom had never had a colourful bonnet in their lifetime. But before Easter, the new Vicar would arrive... and what use would bonnets and dyed eggs be, if the children had nowhere to live?

"I..."

"What have you got to lose? Wouldn't you rather be a wife and mother, than a governess?"

"Yes, er... no, er... I do not know," she broke off, no logical argument coming to her aid. Finally, she nodded her head, "One month. And then I shall have my reference?"

"Yes," Annabelle confirmed. Considering the subject closed, she led Hannah to the stairs, and up to her room. "It's settled then. Now, I suggest that you have that bath and get some sleep. The next few weeks are going to be very busy."

Chapter Five

The days until the promised evening at Almack's seemed drawn out, and Robert found himself utterly frustrated. After the time spent with Lady Hannah, the insipid and rather desperate young women of the *ton* grated on him even more than usual. And he was beginning to wish that he had never invited Marlby to accompany him into the country, for the man was merciless in his teasing, however subtly it was delivered.

Now that a solution to the difficulties caused by his father's Will seemed within his grasp, he wanted to act, to have the whole situation done with, as soon as possible. The fact that to do so required him to now court and convince the lady in question was rather galling when, for so long, women he didn't want had been throwing themselves at him.

Marlby understood those thoughts exactly, and laughed at his grim expression.

"Have another brandy, Tarynholt, and wipe that expression off your face. You'll never win the lady with a look like that!"

Robert glared at his friend.

"And what look will win the lady's approval? When did you become an expert on courting a woman, Marlby?"

Simon had the grace to look a little self-conscious.

"Ah... well... I will admit that my experience is more related to charming ladies, without the intent of matrimony. But the principle is the same. What woman would wish to spend time with a man who does nothing but scowl?"

Robert considered his friend's words and, rather horrifyingly, an image of his father came into his mind, scowling at everything. No wonder his mother had taken herself off to Nettlerush Banks and stayed there. At that thought, he forced himself to relax his face, to smile congenially. There was no possibility that he would allow himself to behave like his father.

"You have a point. It's just that..."

"...you want the matter finalised, and the risk of your cousin ever getting his hands on anything removed."

"Exactly."

"Surely it won't take you too long to convince her – that is, if you've decided, for a certainty, that she will do?"

Robert nodded.

"She will do."

Simon laughed again, and Robert glared.

"I wish you luck then. For I suspect that she'll challenge you, in a way that none of the other possibilities – limited as they are – would ever have done."

"Have you considered, Simon, that I might regard that as a good thing?"

Hannah stepped through the doors of Almack's, nervousness making her hands damp inside her new gloves.

She knew that she looked good, that the blue gown she wore highlighted her sparkling eyes, intensifying their colour, but that did not change just how nervous she felt. Music played as Hannah went with Annabelle around the room, and was introduced to more people than she could ever hope to remember.

Everyone was polite, almost too much so, especially the ladies who had daughters and nieces with them. They smiled with their lips, but not with their eyes, and Hannah's nervousness only seemed to increase as they made their way towards the centre of the large ballroom. She felt completely out of place, as if, somehow, these people were of a different kind entirely from those she had walked amongst all her life.

"How are you feeling, Hannah?"

Annabelle spoke softly, nodding as they passed two older women who had taken seats which afforded them a full view of the dance floor.

"Everyone seems… how shall I put this… curious."

Annabelle laughed lightly.

"That is one way of saying that they are all extremely jealous. You are the newcomer, a surprise that none of them expected, and you are bound to have a full dance card this evening. That colour of blue matches your eyes, and you are a like a breath of fresh air compared to the rest of the women here. Just by existing, you completely destroy all of their plans for marrying their daughters off, and they must reassess everything." She leaned in conspiratorially, "Remember, you promised the first dance to Lord Tarynholt."

Hannah remembered. In fact, as the maids had dressed and prepared her for this evening's Assembly, she'd been able to think of nothing else. The last five days had been filled with trips to Bond Street, gown fittings, trips to the shoemakers, and lessons in dancing and a variety of instruction about how to act amidst the *ton*.

Hannah had found it all very confusing and impossible to remember.

"What if I forget something?"

"I will help you to remember everything. Oh, here is Lord Tarynholt."

Annabelle subtly pointed over Hannah's shoulder and they both turned to watch him, and Lord Marlby, approach.

"Ladies."

Lord Tarynholt bowed to them both, followed by Lord Marlby.

"Gentlemen, how nice to see you here tonight."

Annabelle was perfectly comfortable in the presence of the men, whereas Hannah felt her nervousness redouble at their presence. Lord Tarynholt looked so very handsome in his immaculate evening wear, that he quite took her breath away.

Lord Tarynholt turned his attention to Hannah.

"Lady Hannah, you look much more rested than when last I saw you."

"I am, thank you."

She was blushing, and unable to do anything to stop it.

"Your dance card?"

He held out a gloved hand. It wasn't truly a question – more of a demand, but she didn't even think to deny him. She fumbled with the card, handed it to him, and then watched as he scribbled his name in the spaces for not just one, but the first two dances. She looked up in alarm.

"My Lord?"

"One dance will, I fear, not be enough." He gave her a nod and a smile and then Lord Marlby was taking her dance card and claiming the third dance. When he backed away, Lord Tarynholt addressed her again, "I will return for you in a few moments."

Hannah was stunned speechless and turned to Annabelle after the men left them.

"What just happened?"

Annabelle was beaming, as was Lady Haleston, who had joined them.

"I believe that Lord Tarynholt just declared his intentions, at least where you are concerned. In a manner which will leave no question after tonight."

"But two dances? You told me that was frowned upon unless..." she broke off as she realised exactly what had just occurred. "But... we don't even know one another."

"Precisely why two dances are an excellent idea," Lady Haleston commented.

"He definitely means to pursue you. That is wonderful news, Hannah. Oh, the musicians are getting ready to start. And here comes Lord Tarynholt. Have fun, my dear."

Hannah turned and watched Lord Tarynholt approach her. He bowed, and she curtsied, then he offered her his arm and, as if in a dream, she placed her gloved hand upon it. As he led her to the dance floor and they took up their positions for the country dance, she felt as if she had, somehow, stepped into one of the fairytales she had loved as a child.

Lord Marlby joined them with a lovely young lady who spent the entire dance batting her eyelashes at him and giggling loudly each time she missed a step. Lord Marlby, to his credit, never allowed his smile to falter or his courtesy to slip, but Hannah was thankful that they only joined them for one dance.

"Don't worry about anyone else, you dance wonderfully, Lady Hannah."

Hannah glanced up into Lord Tarynholt's dark blue eyes and smiled.

"Thank you, my Lord. Before coming to London, I had never danced with a partner – your words reassure me, for I had feared to utterly disgrace myself."

"You never danced with the children?"

Hannah shook her head.

"No. A lively game of chase was more our usual sort of activity."

She smiled as she thought of the children, and then sighed, wishing that she knew how everyone was getting on, but she couldn't expect an answer to the letter she'd posted three days ago for at least another few days.

The first dance ended, and she moved to leave the floor, only to find Lord Tarynholt turning her back towards him with a slight touch of his hand on the small of her back. The physical contact brought a soft gasp from her throat as she looked up at him, for that touch, small as it was, had sent heat through her, as if she had been touched by fire. He immediately dropped his hand and nodded.

"I believe the second dance is mine as well."

Hannah looked around at the dowagers and hopeful mothers standing on the sidelines with their eager daughters, and inwardly cringed. Many of them were whispering behind their hands, while their eyes shot daggers in her direction. She did not want to be gossiped about, but it appeared that she had no choice.

"Are you sure that this is a wise thing to do?"

Her voice was barely a whisper.

"I would be offended if you denied me now," he told her. "Come, we are dancing a reel this time. I trust you know the steps?"

Hannah nodded.

"Just barely. I've only just learned." She turned to look at the other side of the room and then gasped at the blatant stares which were focused upon her from the other bachelors who were in attendance. "Everyone is staring at us!"

"They are simply jealous." Lord Tarynholt smiled in amusement. "I, however, am not worried about their stares or their comments. You should not be concerned either."

"I shouldn't?"

"You shouldn't."

The music started and he gently guided her to match his steps. It was a much faster dance than the first, and their conversation faded away as Hannah concentrated hard, to ensure that she avoided a misstep. By the time the musicians finished the tune, she was out of breath and laughing softly.

"That was fun!"

*****

Robert looked at her and thoughts of changing anything about Hannah's behaviour faded away. Everything he had been raised to expect as 'appropriate behaviour' seemed rather stultifying, when compared to the woman before him. She was smiling freely and enjoying herself. She had the same look on her face as she'd had whilst playing with the children, and he discovered that it was a look he hoped to see more often. Society could take their notions of how a young lady was supposed to act and toss them out, as far as he was concerned. He liked this carefree Hannah, and couldn't imagine her trying to conform to the coy, quiet, calculating behaviour which he was used to seeing in the young ladies of the *ton*.

He knew that Lady Hannah had made an agreement with her cousin. He'd spoken with Lord Deerwood, two nights previously at White's, and they had discussed at length the requirements which Lady Hannah had of her future husband. Funding the orphanage was of no consequence for Robert, but it was her first requirement that he'd found puzzling.

She would only marry for love.

"Deerwood, no one of our class marries for such a frivolous reason."

"I'm telling you that she is serious about this, Tarynholt. She isn't even going to consider entering the matrimonial state unless there is love involved. Her parents loved each other – enough that her mother gave up everything to marry the man – and she wants nothing less. Would it be so hard to develop some feelings for her?"

Robert had shaken his head, ignoring the fact that he already had some rather unexpected feelings where the lovely Lady Hannah was concerned. Desire had been at the top of the list. And jealousy. Just the idea that she would be dancing with other gentlemen made him incredibly uncomfortable. Which was why Marlby had consented to claiming her third dance, at his request.

By the fourth dance, he planned to have her walking outside to keep her away from the other eligible Lords of the *ton*. He would use the pretence of getting some fresh air. A light supper would then be served, and there would only be a few dances left after that. He'd already spoken to several of his friends, all of whom had intentions towards other young ladies, and they had agreed to claim her remaining dances.

Seeing her tonight – seeing how well she dealt with being exposed to the eyes of the *ton*, even whilst feeling uncertain, had removed any lingering doubts he had about her suitability. Not only did she meet the requirements of his father's Will, but she also met his own requirement – that of being a person with whom he thought he could bear to spend his life. Now, he planned to convince Viscount Barnsley, whose name was against the last dance on Hannah's dance card, to slip out early, feigning a headache. Robert would then boldly claim the last dance of the evening, shocking the dragons of society, while sealing Hannah's fate firmly in their minds. Two dances might be forgiven, but three? They would be expecting a betrothal before the end of the Season. And he aimed to make sure that happened.

He escorted Hannah back to Lady Deerwood's side, bowing to her and nodding to Marlby as he arrived to take his place, and lead Hannah off to dance. Lady Haleston was waiting for him.

"So? Will she do?"

"She'll do. Did you know that she expects her husband to fund the orphanage in Lower Nettlefold?"

Lady Haleston grinned at him.

"I had heard that. I assume that would not be a problem for you?"

"It is a minor amount of money, compared to the amount I would stand to lose if I do not marry appropriately." He paused and then asked, "Did you know about her other condition?"

Lady Haleston laughed softly.

"Yes. I take it the notion of love doesn't appeal to you?"

Robert was silent for several moments, watching Hannah laugh at something Marlby had said to her. She was beyond lovely, and a fierce sense of possessiveness overtook him.

"I've never given the emotion much thought to be honest. What really is love after all?" He continued to stare at Hannah as he spoke to Lady Haleston. "Although I can't say that I find the concept objectionable."

Lady Haleston smiled as she patted his arm.

"That look in your eye might be lust, not love. And I dare say you shall have to convince the lady to love you as well, my dear Tarynholt. I do not think she is a milquetoast – more likely a challenge. And she may need time. Time that you do not have."

Robert had not even considered the possibility that he would be denied, or that he would be unable to win Hannah over in the short time he needed to fulfil the conditions of his father's Will. He would not allow the possibility of failure – too much depended on him succeeding.

"I thought to take her driving the day after tomorrow. I intend to make my intentions clear at that time."

Lady Haleston smiled again.

"Excellent. I trust that Annabelle is already aware that a wedding will be taking place before she leaves for the country?"

"I'm not sure if she's come to that conclusion, but I trust you will take great pleasure in divulging that information to her."

"Naturally."

"Why do you care about this, Lady Haleston? Why do you take such an interest in her – or in me, for that matter?"

Robert was puzzled about why Lady Haleston was taking such an interest in his personal life, and had felt compelled to ask. He was aware of her reputation for meddling in the lives of the *ton*, but she rarely played such an active role without an ulterior motive.

"I only wish to see two delightful young people happy, my Lord," she replied coyly, and quickly added, "Well, I shall take my leave before the dragons start to gossip about *us*." She tossed her hair as she laughed at the notion that gossip would concern her. "It appears that your intended is becoming a bit overheated. Maybe a short walk in the evening air would serve nicely?"

"My thoughts exactly." He met Hannah as Marlby took his leave and then addressed Lady Deerwood, "I believe that Lady Hannah could do with a breath of fresh air."

"That seems like an excellent idea, Lord Tarynholt. I will see you both during the supper."

She smiled at Hannah and then walked away. From the corner of his eye, Robert saw several eligible gentlemen coming towards them and he took Hannah's elbow and steered her quickly towards the door to the terrace.

"Come this way."

"Is this appropriate?"

She was whispering, glancing around to see if their departure was being noticed.

"As long as we are not gone too long and remain in full view of others, there will be nothing for them to take exception to. You look flushed."

"It is very warm in here."

"Yes it is. Come, we will walk on the terrace for a few minutes. I would like to speak to you further about a private matter, but it can wait until the day after tomorrow. I have appointments tomorrow which cannot be changed."

He pushed the doors open and escorted her out of the building and along the broad terrace, where a few other couples were also taking the air. The sun had set but the lanterns set along the terrace had all been lit, and he made sure to steer Hannah away from the shadows.

Chapter Six

"The day after tomorrow?"

A flutter of butterflies stirred in Hannah's stomach, and she was surprised to realise that she would be counting the hours until that time.

"Yes. I will take you driving in the park."

He didn't ask, Hannah realised – it was as if he simply expected her to agree.

She wasn't sure that she liked that expectation – it was a little overbearing, in a way – yet she chose not to argue it, for she found that she rather wanted his company.

"A drive? In your carriage?"

Hannah knew that she should not ride alone in a closed carriage with a single man.

"No. I have a new phaeton I thought to take out. It being an open carriage, there will be no question of impropriety."

Lord Tarynholt walked beside her, ramrod straight with hands clasped behind his back.

Obviously, he had understood the concern behind her question.

"A phaeton?" she could hear the excitement lacing her voice. "I saw one the other day and they look very grand. And possibly dangerous?"

"Never fear. I promise no harm will come to you while in my company."

He chuckled at her reaction and Hannah smiled at him.

"I shall ask Lady Deerwood's permission then."

She lowered her eyes, aware that it was inappropriate for her to be making arrangements to spend the afternoon with Lord Tarynholt without her cousin's consent. Anything Hannah might do wrongly would reflect badly on her cousin, as her sponsor into society, and she would not like to bring any disapprobation to Annabelle.

"She will agree, I am sure."

Lord Tarynholt spoke confidently, and Hannah nodded.

"I just don't want to embarrass her. She and her husband have been so kind to me."

Lord Tarynholt led her to a bench, surrounded by early spring roses which climbed up the wall of the building, and the thought slipped through her mind that it was a very romantic spot.

"Shall we sit for a few minutes, before going back in for the supper?"

Hannah settled onto the bench, only then realising just how much energy she had expended, dancing.

"That would be pleasant, thank you. I am finding that dancing requires far more effort than I had expected."

They sat for some time, saying little, but somehow comfortable in each other's company, and Hannah allowed her thoughts to wander. But where they wandered surprised her, for she found herself considering what it would be like to spend every day with a man like this....

That thought sent a shiver through her – half fear of the unknown, and half excitement at the possibilities which such a concept presented.

She cast a sideways glance at Lord Tarynholt from under lowered lashes, wondering what he was thinking, only to see that he was watching her, with a smile on his face. Was Annabelle right? Was Lord Tarynholt truly interested in her, as more than a friend?

At that moment, they heard the music end, and Lord Tarynholt rose, holding out his hand to her.

"The supper will be served now – we should go back in."

She took his hand, and allowed him to assist her to her feet, acutely conscious of the heat of his hand, and of the warmth in his gaze when his eyes met hers. Perhaps the next few weeks would be far more pleasant than she had originally expected, when agreeing to Annabelle's request for a month…

* * * * *

As the silence between them extended, Robert found himself comfortable, with no pressing need to fill it with pointless conversation. Instead, he simply watched her. She was beautiful, in a genuine, unaffected way – no artifice was needed to make that beauty obvious, and this evening, she looked stunning in a gown which echoed the soft blue of her eyes.

It would be no hardship to be greeted by her visage every morning…

The scent of the early blooming roses wrapped around them, and the crisp evening air was refreshing after the close feel of the ballroom. When she half turned to regard him from under lowered lashes, he felt the most intense urge to simply bend down and bring his lips to hers.

He forced himself to stay still, for others were not far away, and such an act would be beyond scandalous. But he wanted to do it, wanted to kiss her, more than he had ever wanted to kiss a woman before.

He was saved from the ache of temptation when the music stopped, signalling the supper break, and he rose to lead her back inside.

✳✳✳✳✳

Hannah was exhausted but exhilarated as the last dance of the evening was called, and she looked at her dance card to see the name 'Viscount Barnsley' written on the line - but she could not see the gentleman approaching her. She would not mind sitting this one out if they missed the start of the music.

Lady Haleston reached her side.

"You dance divinely, my dear. Is it true that you only learned the steps this week?"

"Yes, it is. Annabelle insisted that I spend many hours with the dance teacher," Hannah looked around the room in anticipation, then turned back to Lady Haleston, "I think that the gentleman who is to be my partner for the last dance cannot find me – or at least, I do not see him anywhere. Do you know Viscount Barnsley?"

"Oh, what a shame, I fear that I saw the Viscount departing earlier. He was feeling quite poorly."

Lady Haleston's eyes left Hannah's as she peered over the younger woman's left shoulder. Her lips curled slightly upwards in expectation as Hannah heard a soft voice behind her.

"My Lady, would you do me the honour of joining me in the final dance of the evening? I understand that your planned partner has been taken ill." Lord Tarynholt offered his arm to guide her onto the dance floor as the first chord was struck, giving Hannah no opportunity to accept or refuse his invitation. Instinctively, as if it was the most natural thing in the world, she rested her gloved fingertips atop his forearm, even though her mind was instantly in turmoil – what would people say? He inclined his head and leant ever so slightly towards her to whisper, "You look like a vision tonight."

Hannah blushed and bit the inside of her lip as butterflies took flight in her stomach.

"Thank you."

You look very dashing yourself.

But she didn't say the words, feeling that something momentous was happening, that her life was inexorably changed and that she could do nothing to stop that change.

They lined up and began to go through the elaborate steps, their conversation halted for the time being. When the music ended, Lord Tarynholt led her back to Lord and Lady Deerwood, and bid her good evening.

Hannah was still smiling as she threaded her way, following Annabelle and Lord Deerwood, through the throng to reach the exit and out into the cool night air. She ignored the looks sent her way, both by envious young ladies and disapproving dowagers. She hadn't cared what they thought of her before coming to London, and she truly didn't see any reason to care now, especially as Lord Tarynholt did not appear to be concerned about the gossip.

But as the carriage moved through the London streets it was as if a spell had been broken and Hannah was jolted back to reality by every bump of the cobblestones under the wheels. She'd had a wonderful evening, Lord Tarynholt was a handsome gentleman and a delightful dance partner... but Hannah had a goal and a necessary path to take, to get to it.

She would hold to the agreement she'd made with Annabelle, and spend the month enjoying the social events of the Season, but once that month was up, she would have her letter of reference and find a governess position. The orphans were depending upon her, the arrival of the new vicar in Lower Nettlefold was imminent, and she would not be dissuaded from taking care of the orphans, one way or the other.

Hannah clasped her gloved hands in her lap and tried not to cringe, or show any sign on her face of just how awful she found the afternoon's entertainment.

She'd awakened the morning after her first assembly at Almack's to find a large stack of invitations waiting for her.

Annabelle had been thrilled and together, over a cup of tea and some biscuits, they'd opened the invitations and separated them into three piles. The first had been the rejection pile – invitations that no respectable young lady would ever consider accepting. Annabelle had informed her that no reply was necessary for those. The second pile was invitations which were to be politely declined, for one reason or another.

The third pile was the one which concerned Hannah the most. The invitations to be accepted. A written note needed to be sent to each person, notifying them that Hannah and Annabelle would be attending their dinner, or tea or soiree. The number of events seemed staggering to Hannah, but Annabelle had suggested that this was only the beginning and that, as she'd made such an impression the night before, she could expect twice as many the next day. Hannah was completely overwhelmed, but she trusted Annabelle's advice and simply did what Annabelle suggested.

The first event was a musicale, to be held at Eversby House that same afternoon. Annabelle had already been scheduled to attend, and after meeting Hannah at Almack's the previous evening, Lady Beatrice Eversby had insisted that the newest member of society be brought along to hear her sing.

Annabelle had suggested a day dress in a delicate mint green colour as the perfect attire for the afternoon's excursion and Hannah had allowed herself to be dressed and groomed by the maids once again. Now, as Lady Beatrice Eversby strained to hit a note considerably above her range, Hannah forced herself to look as if she was not finding the singing painful. The screeching – which Lady Beatrice believed to be singing - had been ongoing for almost an hour now, and Hannah surreptitiously glanced around, to see that everyone else in attendance was trying to keep their composure as well, with varying degrees of success.

She breathed a momentary sigh of relief when this latest vocal disaster concluded, only to mentally groan when yet another piece was announced.

Hannah tried to remember what Annabelle had told her about endurance and proper behaviour, but when Lady Beatrice launched into a note which shook the walls and caused pain in her ears, she could bear it no longer. Something had to be done to stop this torturous debacle. Using a distraction which the orphans had often employed, she surged to her feet, her chair clattering as it fell over while she clutched her throat, coughing and gagging in a most horrendous fit.

Gasps from everyone in the room ensued, and Annabelle came to her aid, patting her lightly on the back and peering into her face, attempting to identify the source of her distress. Lady Beatrice even came over and patted her back a moment or two, exclaiming her concern loudly.

"The poor dear, she was so overcome by the song."

Overcome with fright maybe.

Hannah accepted their help, calming down only after she saw the musician, who had been playing the pianoforte to accompany Lady Beatrice, leave the room. Then, sure of reprieve, she miraculously recovered and asked to be placed where she could regain her composure in quiet, before enjoying the rest of the recital.

"Oh, I wouldn't want you to become overwhelmed again," Lady Beatrice informed her. "I think my voice needs a slight rest anyway."

At that, Lady Beatrice's mother hurried to speak to the other guests.

"There are refreshments on the terrace. Please enjoy yourselves."

Hannah dabbed at her forehead with a handkerchief while Annabelle fussed over her, making sure that Lady Beatrice knew she didn't need to stay and that she and Hannah would join the others in a few minutes. Once Lady Beatrice was gone, Annabelle burst into laughter.

"That was awful of you."

Hannah gave her an innocent look.

"Whatever are you talking about? My ears were getting ready to bleed."

She could not contain a giggle, causing Annabelle to join in again. Annabelle finally repressed her laughter, and spoke with a more serious expression.

"There are times when I wish I could ignore certain invitations, but the Eversby family is not one to offend. Lady Beatrice imagines herself famous for her singing one day, and has engaged a private tutor for two seasons now. I'm sad to say that her vocal talents have not improved with age."

A sound at the door caused both women to look up and smile.

"Kitty! I didn't know you would be attending."

"Fashionably late as usual," lowering her voice, she added, "have I managed to escape the performance?" Hannah blushed as Annabelle recounted the actions which had halted Lady Beatrice's recital earlier than anticipated. When she was finished, Lady Haleston smiled. "Good for you. Why don't Hannah and I go for a walk and meet you in the gardens? You can let our hostess know that we are taking her home to rest."

"A very good idea."

Annabelle smiled, pleased to see Kitty taking an interest in her cousin's well-being. Lady Haleston led Hannah out into the gardens.

"So I understand that Lord Tarynholt will be taking you driving tomorrow?"

Hannah nodded.

"That is what he said. He wishes to speak with me."

"Yes, I imagine he does, after last night's display."

"Display?"

Hannah regarded her in confusion.

"Three dances in one night. What was that man thinking?" Lady Haleston slipped Hannah's arm through her own and led her along a pathway lined with colourful flowers. "Well, what's done is done. You and Robert will do well together."

"My Lady?"

70

Hannah stopped walking and looked at Lady Haleston, uncertain that she understood the full meaning of her words.

"Lord Tarynholt is a tremendous catch. There are many young ladies hoping he might notice them, and he has chosen you. You have done well for yourself, and you've only just arrived," explained Lady Haleston. "Oh – here is Annabelle - if you'll excuse me, I shall make my farewells to our hostess before joining you and Annabelle at the carriage."

As Annabelle approached her, Hannah stood for a moment on the path, pondering what Lady Haleston had implied. This was all moving so fast. All she wanted to do was prove herself to her mother's family, so that she might receive a letter of reference to be a governess, and earn enough money to take care of herself, with a little left over to help the children at the orphanage. The thought of them made her heart ache - how she did miss them! She wished that she could be with them now and not in the midst of London society, pretending to be something she was not. But, if they were to have anywhere to live, it was up to her to somehow find a way...

She had no idea how she had so quickly become the potential bride of an Earl, and one considered among the most eligible bachelors of the Season. She would have to try to slow things down with Lord Tarynholt. He was certainly attractive and enjoyable to be with, in fact, he caused the most interesting sensations in her, when he was near... but she would need time to get to know him, to discover if there was truly a mutual attraction which could possibly become love. Marriage was not something to be decided within weeks of meeting.

Although... she did not really have much more than weeks, if she was to solve the problems of supporting the orphans...

Annabelle had been waylaid by an older lady, and stopped to talk to her, so Hannah simply stood there, close to the hedge, waiting. As she did, she heard voices coming through the hedge beside her, no doubt from some of the other guests who were also clearing their heads with some fresh air after the dreadful performance. She had just turned to walk away, for she had no interest in eavesdropping on the women, when she was stopped in her tracks by the mention of Lord Tarynholt's name.

"I cannot believe that he is back in London already and did not call on me. I did not attend Almack's last night because I thought that he would not be there."

The petulant whine no doubt belonged to a younger woman, from the timbre of the voice.

"From what I was told, he was quite occupied last evening and would not have given you the time of day anyway."

The second woman sounded to be clearly older, and far more haughty.

"Nonsense! Whatever you heard, his attention to one of the other young women can only be fleeting. It cannot last. I happen to be aware of some very specific requirements which Lord Tarynholt has for his bride, and I also know that I am the only one who can fulfil them. I was under the clear understanding that we would be betrothed before Easter."

The older woman clucked her tongue, and when she spoke, there was unmistakable gloating pleasure in her voice.

"Actually, Lady Marigold, rumour has it that the young woman who held Lord Tarynholt's attention last night fulfils his requirements as well."

The younger woman's only response was a strangled cry of anger.

Hannah felt guilty for listening, but was transfixed by their words. What did the women mean about Lord Tarynholt's requirements? Who was Lady Marigold? Clearly she was someone who anticipated a betrothal from Lord Tarynholt.

Given what she had just heard, Hannah was now anxious to see Lord Tarynholt the following day, but she was not going to join him for a drive, in public, as he had wanted. He may wish to speak to her, but now, she had questions of her own which she wanted answered.

Questions which she pondered as Annabelle finally reached her, and they went to the carriage.

Chapter Seven

It was not long past dawn when Hannah awoke, exhausted from a fitful night, and with a dull headache. As she rubbed the sleep from her eyes, she recalled the strange conversation she had overheard the previous day, about requirements which Lord Tarynholt had for a wife. Her apprehension came flooding back, and she knew that she would have to ask him about the matter directly, especially after the way in which he had showered her with attention at Almack's, before any more rumours started swirling around the *ton*.

But she really had no right to question him about what she'd overheard. Perhaps she should ask Annabelle or Kitty what to do. In the meantime, she would refuse any further public outings with Lord Tarynholt until she found out more about what the women she'd overheard had meant.

Because what they had said completely confused her, as it had, she'd come to realise, implied that she, herself, met whatever those mysterious requirements were. How was that possible?

*****

Hannah was enjoying a light brunch with Annabelle, and was just building up her courage to ask Annabelle about what she'd overheard in the garden the previous day, when Milton announced the arrival of a visitor.

"Lord Marlby to see Lady Hannah, my Lady."

"Do show him in, please."

Moments later he was shown into the parlour, where he bowed to the ladies who had risen to greet him.

"I do hope that you've enjoyed your first weeks in London, Lady Hannah?"

Hannah smiled.

"It's all so new, and exhausting, but yes I have. It feels so far away from my life in Lower Nettlefold."

Lord Marlby nodded in understanding.

"Actually, I am here to speak of Lower Nettlefold. I will be traveling through there on a journey which will begin tomorrow. Is there anything which you would like me to bring back for you?"

"You're going to Lower Nettlefold?"

Hannah felt a tug at her heart at the thought. Lord Marlby nodded.

"Just beyond it actually, to my estate between Upper Nettlefold and Bath, but I would be close enough to stop by on my return journey should you require anything in the area."

"That is so kind of you." Hannah debated, internally, whether she should ask for such a favour, but found the opportunity too compelling to let pass. "Actually, do you remember the orphanage where you and Lord Tarynholt found me? The day that I met you for the first time?"

"Of course. Was there something you needed from there?"

"Just word that everyone is doing well."

"Ah... is there reason that you might expect them not to be?"

Hannah saw Lord Marlby's confusion, and so explained her concern.

"The manor house which is used for the orphanage was originally the vicarage. When my father was vicar, he saw no need for us to occupy such a large home when there were children in need. So, he declared that it should be used as the orphanage while my parents and I lived in the verger's cottage. But the new vicar who will replace my father has seven children, and I know that he will need the manor house. He is not scheduled to arrive in Lower Nettlefold until early April, but I worry that he may have sent ahead, and demanded that the children be relocated early. And I must confess that, at this juncture, I do not know where they can be moved to, for I know of no other building which is both suitable and available, not to mention affordable. It is too soon to have had a response to any of my letters, but knowing that the vicar is due to arrive soon, I have been concerned while awaiting some news."

Lord Marlby smiled, tilted his head, and considered her.

"I would be happy to stop and check on the children and their caretakers. I will be gone several weeks, but I will bring you word upon my return."

Hannah's eyes glistened with unshed tears, and she smiled sincerely.

"Thank you so much, that is very kind. I feel better already, and I hope that my worry is unfounded."

"I will make it my purpose to bring only good news upon my return then," Lord Marlby told her, and she felt the sincerity in his words.

✹✹✹✹✹

"My Lady, Lord Tarynholt has arrived."

Hannah glanced up at the maid and gave her a wan smile.

"Thank you. I'll be down shortly."

Annabelle had gone to tea with Lady Haleston, and wasn't planning to return until late in the afternoon. Between Lord Marlby's short visit, and Annabelle leaving to make her calls, Hannah had not been able to find the right moment to ask Annabelle about the conversation she had overheard, and her resulting confusion. Now, she was faced with a difficult decision.

After some thought, she concluded that she should tell Lord Tarynholt that she was not feeling well enough to accompany him for a drive in his phaeton, and beg his indulgence to simply allow her to rest, suggesting that he call again on another day. Hopefully, he would take his leave quickly, and she would be able to avoid any further conversation with him until she'd had a chance to speak to Annabelle, and decide how she felt about the situation.

Hannah went to the wash basin and splashed some of the water onto her face, before taking the cloth and patting it dry. Her eyes looked tired, but she felt no desire to mask this from her visitor.

She descended the stairs and stepped into the parlour quietly, leaving the door open so that the maid who waited in the hallway could see them, and propriety would be maintained. She paused and watched the man standing near the windows. He was tall, his shoulders were broad, and his legs solid beneath the cloth of his fawn breeches. His tall Hessian boots were polished perfectly, and the blue waistcoat he wore almost matched the deep blue of his eyes. He was, more than ever, handsome enough to quite steal her breath, despite the doubt which had filled her, ever since she had overheard that peculiar conversation.

After some time, it seemed that he sensed her eyes upon him, and he turned, a ready smile upon his lips. She swallowed and stepped forward, her excuse tumbling from her lips.

"I'm sorry but I'm unable to go driving with you today."

Lord Tarynholt searched her face for a moment.

"You are unwell?"

"I have a headache - nothing a day of rest won't cure."

That is, if I can forget what I overheard yesterday long enough to fall asleep.

"We do not have to drive today. Why don't we go and sit in the garden for a while? The day is quite warm, and I need to speak with you about a delicate matter."

Hannah raised a brow and considered refusing his request, opting instead to confront him as a surge of frustrated confusion filled her.

"More delicate than the fact that you claimed three dances with me at Almack's so that I should become the centre of attention and the subject of gossip and rumours within mere days of my arrival in London?"

Lord Tarynholt grinned at her and then immediately wiped the smile from his face, apparently sensing the gravity of the situation from her perspective. She wished, in that instant, that the ways of society were not so complex, and so layered in politeness rather than direct honesty. She did not know how to dissemble, truly.

"What I wish to discuss involves that and more."

Hannah sighed.

"You acted deliberately that first night, knowing that there would be consequences." It was a statement, not a question. In the short time that she'd known Lord Tarynholt, he'd not struck her as the type of man who acted impulsively. He'd known full well what dancing three times with her at Almack's would mean. Kitty had explained that, should a betrothal announcement not be made in the next few weeks, it would be her reputation which suffered, not his. "I should have known to refuse that last dance," Hannah murmured to herself, as she considered how she might protect her tender heart and her reputation. "Were you trying to test how well I had learned the rules of society? Did you wish to embarrass me?"

"Of course not, dear Lady Hannah. And I would not have let you refuse the last dance." He obviously hoped for a smile from her, but that hope was to no avail. He regarded her stern expression and sighed. "Come, we'll sit in the garden and discuss this where the servants cannot overhear."

Hannah, seeing that she had no other choice, inclined her head, and led the way towards the rear door, and the gardens beyond. The maid trailed after them, and at the door, Hannah turned to her, conscious of the need to maintain propriety even while wishing for privacy.

"Please wait here, Mary, where you can see us, but still allow us some privacy to converse."

"Yes, my Lady."

The maid bobbed a curtsey, and Hannah smiled at her, then turned and stepped out into the garden. The sun was shining, brightly enough to hurt her eyes because of her megrim, and she immediately went to a bench which was situated beneath a large tree. She sighed gratefully as she settled in the shade.

Lord Tarynholt sat next to her, so close that mere inches separated their thighs. She could feel the heat of his body, and despite her misgivings, a flutter of excitement twisted in her stomach. She tried to put a little more distance between them, but doing so put her in danger of falling off the end of the rather small bench, so she stopped, and concentrated on what they might say, trying to ignore the closeness of him, the scent of his cologne, and the pounding of her heart.

"You understand that by dancing with you three times that first night I have effectively declared my intention to offer for your hand?"

"Yes, and you have placed me in a most delicate situation by doing so. Lord Tarynholt, why would you do that? We hardly know one another."

"Do you believe in fate, Lady Hannah?"

She considered his question for a moment.

"Possibly. Why do you ask?"

"From the moment I met you, I felt we were destined to become man and wife," he said. "You see, it is time for me to marry and start a family. Now that my father has died, I have a duty to carry on the family name and title."

"But why me?"

Lord Tarynholt lowered his eyes.

"You may have noticed that many eligible young women have been vying for my attention." He glanced up at her, but she kept her expression impassive. "But not one of them meets my requirements for marriage."

Hannah trembled.

He was going to be honest with her. Lady Marigold was right – he did have requirements, and it seemed that he was going to tell her about them. But what could those requirements be, that she could fulfil?

*****

Robert hesitated as he considered how much to reveal. He did care for Lady Hannah, and he believed that she would make a good wife for him. He believed that they would grow to love one another in time. But he was not completely certain of his feelings right now – he cared for her more than he ever had for any other woman, but was that enough to label it 'love'? He was not at all certain. But he did not want to offend her, or frighten her away.

"In a society where marriages are arranged primarily based on convenience," he began, "I have decided that this is not enough for me. My requirement is that I will only marry for love." Hannah gasped. Robert gazed intently into her eyes and took her hand. "What do you say, my Lady? Would you do me the honour of becoming my wife?"

Hannah returned his stare for a long moment before responding. Then she slipped her hand from his, and his heart pounded – surely she would not refuse him? He might not have said that he loved her – for he could not bring himself to baldly make that statement yet – but he had implied... She met his eyes, and swallowed, hesitating a bare moment before speaking.

"I have my own requirements for marriage, my Lord. I have a moral obligation to the children of the orphanage. If I cannot work as a governess to earn money to take care of their needs, then I will require my husband to fund their care."

"Done," he said simply. "Is that all?"

Her eyes widened and he laughed.

"Do you really mean it? You will provide funding for the orphanage?"

She sounded both delighted and disbelieving.

"Yes, my dear, I will. Whatever makes you happy."

He took her hands again, pulled her up from the bench, and twirled her around in the garden. In that moment, he was filled with a rush of relief – and not just relief that he would be able to fulfil the conditions of his father's Will, but relief, that his growing feelings for her would not be denied.

He wanted her to want him, to a rather shocking degree.

✷✷✷✷✷

Hannah's heart was pounding so hard in her chest that she felt dizzy. Was Lord Tarynholt actually telling her that he loved her? She knew that she had feelings for him, desires which frightened her. But could either of them actually feel real love, having only just met?

And yet... he sounded sincere, and he had just promised her the one thing she most wanted (apart from love, that was) – the guarantee of care for the orphans. Could she, in any reasonable manner, refuse him? Did she even want to? Given her own growing feelings for him, surely she would be quite mad if she did.

She looked almost coyly at the man who would imminently be declared her betrothed.

"I'm sorry if this sounds forward of me, but I am quite concerned for the well-being of the children, since the new vicar may take over the manor house within a week or so. Could we please see to their care immediately?"

"Yes, of course we can."

"Then yes, Lord Tarynholt, I will marry you, if that is truly what you wish."

He smiled then, a smile which lit his face to a brilliance which set her heart pounding even harder.

"Thank you! Do not think of worrying about the orphans again. I will have my man of business take care of it at once. You will have enough to take care of to plan a wedding - I would propose that we wed before Lady Deerwood retires to the country for her confinement. We should just have time for the banns to be read."

✳✳✳✳✳

A week later, the betrothal of Robert, Lord Tarynholt, and Lady Hannah Charteris was announced at a grand evening at the home of Lord and Lady Deerwood. Hannah wore an emerald-green gown, and her hair was woven with gold threads and piled elegantly atop her head. An emerald necklace completed the stunning effect.

She was breath-taking and Robert could not take his eyes off his betrothed. With both Hannah's parents and Robert's parents deceased, Robert had chosen to keep the event small, and for close friends only. He was disappointed that Marlby had not yet returned from his journey, but was certain that he'd be forgiven for not awaiting his closest friend's return before making the announcement. The only blight on the evening was that, although Robert would have preferred he not be invited, his cousin Herbert was also in attendance, as it would not have been proper to shun him – doing so would have created a storm of gossip, which he very much wanted to avoid.

Herbert sneered in Robert's direction as he spoke to Lady Haleston, who was observing the room from a corner, visibly pleased with herself for her matchmaking prowess.

Robert wondered what thoughts were going through his cousin's mind, for surely the man was seething with anger, given that now, he would never inherit the funds or the unentailed properties. He shuddered at the thought of Herbert's attitudes, knowing that, by marrying him, Hannah was saving so many people from Herbert's clutches. How Lady Haleston could bear to speak to the man was beyond him – but he was grateful for her distracting the scoundrel. He turned his attention back to Hannah, resolving to let nothing spoil the day.

✳✳✳✳✳

Kitty regarded the man beside her with barely concealed disgust. Still, inside, part of her exulted, pleased beyond measure that her plans had come to fruition.

"I know you had something to do with his," Herbert said to her through clenched teeth. "I will find a way to make you pay, if it is the last thing I do."

"You can no longer harm me, you snivelling imbecile. I suggest that you compose your expression, and accept your fate. Unless, of course, you intend to cause a scene, and give the gossips even more fodder to work with?"

Herbert ground his teeth, and his gaze might have made a lesser woman quail, but Kitty simply fixed a stiff smile onto her face and waited. Moments later, Herbert sighed, and made his own expression carefully blank, lest any of the other guests look in their direction. Obviously, he did not wish to be the subject of any more gossip than he already was.

"Rest assured, my dear Katherine, I will not forget, nor will I forgive. In the end, you will pay."

"I do not think that I am the one whose behaviour requires retribution, Herbert. Far from it. And I suggest that you remember what I know about your past, before you attempt to take any action against me – or against those I care for."

Herbert glared at her, grinding his teeth in frustration, but he said nothing more. Which was surprisingly wise of him, Kitty thought.

Chapter Eight

Hannah was radiant and relaxed as she accepted congratulations from the guests. While she had finally learned to enjoy the Soirees, Balls, and the whirl of activities in London somewhat, even looking forward to donning the beautiful gowns and dancing, she was relieved to know that such frivolous pursuits would not necessarily be required of her in her new life as the Countess of Tarynholt. Shortly after she had accepted his proposal, Lord Tarynholt had surprised Hannah by asking her if she would mind terribly if they spent most of their time living at his country estate.

"I spend as little time in London as I can. I prefer the quiet and the wide-open fields of the country, my horses, and the gardens," he explained. "I hate to deprive you of the social whirl which you deserve as a Countess, but would you be willing to spend most of our time in the country?"

Hannah couldn't help the smile which had formed on her face.

"I don't know how people do this for months on end." She had said, visibly relieved. "Do you know how long it takes to get dressed and have my hair done for an evening out? Longer than the evening itself. I do so miss the simple life in the country."

In that moment, Robert realised that any doubt in his mind that he was marrying for love had been quashed by the kind, generous and caring nature of his betrothed. Each day he grew more and more fond of her, not to mention his growing desire for her. Perhaps he was beginning to understand what love was, after all.

✻✻✻✻✻

Once all of the guests had departed, and they could finally seek their beds, Annabelle sent the maid to bed herself, after the long day, and told her that she would help Hannah change into her night attire. She wanted to hear how Hannah was coping, after the whirlwind of activity and the attention which she had received. Hannah was now the most talked about and envied lady of the Season, having become betrothed to Lord Tarynholt.

Hannah threw her arms around her cousin and held her in a warm embrace.

"Thank you, my dear cousin, for everything you have done for me," she said. "I never would have believed that, in such short time, my life would change so, and that I could be happy again."

"And I am happy for you, Hannah," said Annabelle. "Lord Tarynholt will make a fine husband. And I trust that he meets your requirements?"

Annabelle winked at her impressionable charge as she stood behind her to carefully remove the pins and gold threads from her hair, and then brush it.

"And I, his."

Hannah blushed at this revelation.

"Oh!" Annabelle lowered the brush and looked at Hannah in the mirror. "He has told you about his requirements and you find them acceptable?"

"Why, of course," Hannah regarded Annabelle, confused as to why Annabelle thought that she might not be happy with her betrothed expressing his desire to marry for love, just as she did. "Why would I not?"

"I know you have found it difficult to come to terms with the ways of London society, and the notion that for most of the peers, a marriage of convenience is regarded as most sensible, but I am sure that Lord Tarynholt will be a good husband and grow to care fondly for you as time goes by. My marriage to George was arranged, and I hardly knew him when we wed, but we grew quite fond of one another. It does not matter one wit that Lord Tarynholt has to marry quickly to meet the terms of his father's Will."

Hannah turned on her stool and stared at Annabelle.

"Wha... what are you saying?"

Hannah watched as Annabelle realised that something was amiss, and it became obvious to both of them that Lord Tarynholt had not revealed the whole truth to Hannah. Whatever that whole truth was, which Annabelle appeared to know...

"Oh, Hannah, do not be concerned. He cares for you, I know it. I can see it in his eyes."

Hannah's looked at her cousin with horror, and her heart twisted in her breast as she became aware that her betrothed was not the man she had thought he was. For the man she had believed him to be would have told her the truth. Certainly, he had not actually said 'I love you' to her, but he had very clearly implied it. An implication which, it seemed, was a lie.

"Tell me the truth, Annabelle. I want to know everything."

Annabelle took her hand, and led her to the bed, dropping down to sit upon it beside her. The clock ticked on the mantel, as if marking the time until Hannah's hopes would all be destroyed. Annabelle met her eyes, and sighed, quite clearly struggling to find the right words.

Hannah waited, her mouth dry, and her hands shaking as she twisted them together.

"Tarynholt is a good man. His father was less so. His father, in fact, could be described, even if one was being charitable, as having been an irascible controlling bear of a man. So much so that Lady Tarynholt chose, many years ago, to live permanently at their estate near Bath – Nettlerush Banks – and Robert, once he had completed his time at Cambridge, chose to reside there with her. Lady Tarynholt stayed there until her death, refusing to see her husband. His father did everything he could in life to control his son – and Robert resisted that control at all times."

Hannah considered those words carefully.

"But… if that is the case, what could he do, in his Will – surely, once dead, his ability to enforce his will upon anyone was removed?"

"That is the sad part. For he succeeded in death as he never had in life. He set a stricture upon Robert receiving the unentailed properties, and all of the funds held in various banks. A very simple clause, which, unless met, would mean that Robert would have the title and the entailed properties, but not the wherewithal to maintain them. All of that wealth would go to Robert's cousin, if the clause is not met – and the cousin is not a pleasant man. You met him, today – Mr Herbert Calthorpe."

Hannah shuddered.

"He was a very unpleasant man indeed! But what is the exact requirement that the Will set?"

Annabelle patted her hand gently.

"That Robert must marry before then end of one year's time after his mourning ended, and that the woman he marries must be the daughter of an Earl, a Marquess, or a Duke. That year will be up at the end of May. And of all of the eligible young ladies in London this year, only one, other than you, is the daughter of a man of high enough title to fulfil that requirement."

Hannah stared at Annabelle for a moment, then turned and dove face down onto her pillows in anguish, and wept.

Suddenly, that conversation which she had overheard made sense – dreadful sense. The younger woman must have been the only other eligible young lady who met those requirements.

"He lied to me! He does not love me. I will not marry him!"

"Hannah, it is too late to turn back now," said Annabelle. "You would never survive a broken betrothal. You will be ostracised."

"I do not care," she wailed. "I did not want to marry in the first place. Please, you must give me the letter of reference you promised. I shall be a governess and return to the children of the orphanage. I shall never marry."

Annabelle sat beside her and stroked her hair.

"'Tis not so simple, my dear," she said. "Do you not understand? Neither the granddaughter of an Earl, nor the daughter of a Duke is so easily placed as a governess."

"I might as well not be the granddaughter of an Earl," Hannah sniffed. "He has not even acknowledged me."

"Get some sleep," said Annabelle. "Things will not seem so grim in the morning. At least Lord Tarynholt agreed to fund the orphanage. He does care for you, Hannah, you will see."

Hannah turned away from Annabelle, knowing that her words were wise, but not wishing to hear them, regardless.

Annabelle extinguished the candle and closed the door softly behind her as she exited Hannah's room, devastated to hear the sobs as she retreated to her own chamber.

More tears came to Hannah then, once Annabelle had left the room, but despite her despair at it all, a thought wound itself through her mind – if Lord Tarynholt did not marry a woman who met the conditions set out in his father's Will, how many tenants and servants on his estates would suffer, if there were no funds to support things?

And why had he not simply married that other woman? Although… that woman – Lady Marigold? – had not sounded at all pleasant.

Could it be that, by marrying Lord Tarynholt, Hannah would be not only saving him from a miserable marriage, but also saving those dependent on him from starvation and more?

If that was the case, then it would be selfish of her to refuse to go through with the wedding.

*****

"My Lady, I protest, I did not lie to you," Robert insisted. "I am sorry that I did not reveal all of the details of my father's Will, but I did not think it relevant any longer. My feelings for you far outweighed any further thoughts of marrying only to comply with the requirements of his directive."

Before him, Lady Hannah sat, her expression one of great disbelief. When he had called, expecting everything between them to be happy, as it had been the previous evening, he had been shocked to be greeted coldly. But once she had, in a manner which he had come to realise was typical of her, come straight to the point, and demanded an explanation from him, of why he had 'lied to her', his heart had sunk.

Now, he was trying to convince her of the truth of his motivations. And even as he defended himself, guilt filled him. Until she had confronted him with so much distress in her voice, until he, his own heart now irrevocably involved in the matter, he had not, truly, understood how much hurt could come from simply not telling someone all that there was to be told on a matter. If he had understood before, he would have told her all of it, from the start.

She met his gaze, her blue eyes glittering with unshed tears, and his heart broke within him. He wanted to pull her into his arms, to reassure her, but he was quite certain that, should he try to do so, she would push him away.

"How can I believe you, when you did not tell me anything of this?"

He swallowed, his mouth dry, fearing that she might utterly reject him, and not knowing quite what to say.

"I... I suppose that I cannot expect you to trust me – but can you permit me to prove that I care for you? Will you at least allow us some time together, so that you can see my feelings displayed?"

She looked away for a moment, drawing in a deep breath, then brought her eyes back to his.

"I will. Rest assured that I will not reject our betrothal – although I did consider doing so. For the sake of both our reputations, as well as for the orphans, I will continue. But know that I am not at all happy with what you have done. I may, in fact, never forgive you."

✱✱✱✱✱

The early spring day was unseasonably warm, causing Annabelle and Hannah to choose to walk to take tea at Kitty's townhouse, rather than take the carriage. Two footmen followed them as they walked. The sun was bright, and trees were greening quickly, following the rains of the previous few days, the air refreshing as they strolled along the edge of Hyde Park.

The wedding of Hannah and Lord Tarynholt was only days away and Hannah was still heartsick from his deception, despite his attempts to convince her that his feelings were true. He had sent flowers to her every day, after the confrontation she'd had with him following Annabelle's revelation on the evening that they had announced their betrothal.

He had been insistent that he wished to marry her, more because of his growing feelings for her, than because of his father's Will. Hannah had not believed him when he'd said it, and she still did not believe it, no matter that he continued to protest it to be so, but she also realised that her options were limited. Kitty had implored her to heed Annabelle's warnings and proceed with the wedding.

Part of today's visit for tea was, she was sure, so that Kitty could convince her that love came in many forms, and was expressed in a variety of ways – as she had been trying to do, since that horrible revelation.

Upon their arrival, the butler showed Hannah and Annabelle into the pretty day parlour near the back of the house, where large windows overlooked the garden. Looking out, Hannah noticed a gentleman sitting on a bench amongst the flowers, with a blanket over his knees, but before she had a chance to ask Annabelle about him, Kitty greeted them.

"My dear ladies." She embraced first Annabelle then Hannah, taking the younger woman's hands in her own. "The big day is near, how are you feeling?"

"I am as well as can be expected."

Hannah spoke carefully, although her meek voice betrayed her, as did her downturned gaze.

"Before we sit down to tea, I hoped that you would say good day to my husband. He is well enough today to sit in the garden, and has been anxious to meet you."

"The Marquess?"

Hannah had heard so many different rumours about the Marquess of Haleston that she was immediately apprehensive about the unexpected meeting. Politeness would not allow her to refuse, however, and she allowed Kitty to guide her through the French doors to the garden. Hannah turned around to look at Annabelle imploringly, but her cousin encouraged her to proceed without an audience.

"Darling," Kitty spoke gently to the Marquess, a grey-haired, shrivelled man who was at least twice her age, and looked older. "Our dear Hannah has come to meet you."

She drew Hannah closer so that she stood directly in front of the pale gentleman as he slowly raised his head. Hannah curtsied tentatively.

"My Lord, it is an honour to meet you."

"Lady Hannah."

The Marquess slurred her name, one side of his face and mouth drooping lower than the other, as he met her eyes. Hannah froze in place, startled as she looked directly into the eyes of Kitty's husband.

A vague sense of recognition tingled in her breast. She knew these eyes. These were the eyes of her mother. Hannah stared for a moment, speechless, and then turned to Kitty with a questioning look.

Kitty smiled and nodded.

"Yes, Hannah, this is your grandfather, who was once the Earl of Scartmoor – a title which his son now holds, since the time that my husband inherited the Marquessate."

At that moment, Annabelle joined them and, after a reassuring squeeze of Hannah's shoulders, crouched down in front of the Marquess.

"Uncle, you look well today."

"Hmm, the sun helps," he said. "Kitty has told me of your kindness to Hannah. Thank you for taking care of my granddaughter."

Hannah watched, her mind in turmoil as a tangle of emotions filled her. Here was the man who had cast her mother off, for daring to love someone he did not approve of – she should be angry with him. But now, seeing him so reduced, and hearing the sadness in his voice, she could not find it in her. Instead, she felt the anger, which she had carried since the day that her mother had told her of it all, fading away.

The past was the past, and nothing could change it.

Annabelle touched the Marquess' hand again, and spoke softly.

"It has been my honour to do so, Uncle. She has done well – you should be proud of her. It is a pity that her mother is not here to see how beautiful her child is, and how well she carries herself amongst society."

At Annabelle's words, the Marquess closed his eyes, and a spasm of what Hannah thought was grief crossed his face.

Then he opened them again, and looked at Hannah.

"I am glad to hear, granddaughter, that you do so well. But now I tire. Perhaps you will visit me again?"

Hannah stepped forward, and, as Annabelle had done, crouched down to bring her eyes level with his.

"Grandfather... if I may call you so... thank you. I have long wanted to meet you. I am glad to have done so now."

He smiled – a lopsided smile, as the muscles of his face refused to completely obey him, but the smile was in his eyes as well, and he lifted a shaking hand to gently touch her face, before letting it drop back into his lap, as if even that movement exhausted him.

Hannah stood, and stepped back, just as a maid interrupted discreetly to tell Kitty that the tea had been served. The ladies retreated indoors and, over tea, Annabelle and Kitty explained to Hannah how her grandfather had come to be the Marquess of Haleston and Kitty's husband. The Marquess stayed in the garden, but Hannah promised to return after tea and sit with him for a while, if he felt well enough.

Chapter Nine

As they sipped tea, Kitty told Hannah the fascinating story of how she had become the Marchioness of Haleston.

Ten years earlier, Kitty was a commoner, Miss Katherine Thompson, a governess in the home of Baron Reville, none other than the stepfather of Herbert, Lord Tarynholt's cousin. Kitty was a beauty and was forever fighting off the advances of her employer. She did her best to ensure that she was never alone with Baron Reville, yet he would reach for her, and touch her inappropriately whenever he could. His repulsive threats, whispered in her ear whenever he pressed himself against her, promised that he would soon have her exactly where and how he desired. She lived in constant fear of being caught alone, and unable to retreat from his overtures. What made it worse was the fact that, over time, Herbert began to regard her in the same manner.

One day she had entered the Baron's private study to collect the stuffed bear of her charge, who would not settle down to sleep without her favourite cuddle toy, carefully ensuring that the room was vacant before doing so. As she retrieved the toy, she heard the voices of Baron Reville and Herbert approaching, so she slipped behind the drapery to avoid detection, for to be trapped in the Baron's study by both men would no doubt end in disaster for her.

"This is excellent, Herbert," said the Baron. "I do believe that your idea will work. We only need to falsify one document to change the rightful heir to the Marquess of Haleston, so that I should gain the title on his death. After all, who is to say that the midwife did not make a mistake? Neither my grandmother, nor the midwife still lives, so it becomes a matter of hearsay. I am certain that my father must have been the first twin to greet the world, and that things were simply written down incorrectly. This is obviously a matter of correcting an accidental error. You will be well rewarded for your efforts in this matter."

"Thank you, stepfather," said Herbert. "The Earl of Scartmoor does not deserve to inherit the Marquessate. He is a miserable shell of a man and not fitting to hold such a title and high honour. He will also not stand in our way as he is unaware of his standing in this matter, because he keeps to himself, not mixing in society since his wife's death. As a consequence, I do not believe that he has any knowledge of his cousin's frail state of health."

"It should always have been my father who became Earl – he was a far better man than Scartmoor. And if he had, then I would be Earl of Scartmoor today."

"At least, stepfather, your service to the Crown was recognised with the grant of the Barony."

Reville had shaken his head.

"What is a mere Barony, compared to an Earldom, or a Marquessate?"

Kitty had continued to listen as Baron Reville and his stepson, Herbert, detailed their plans to steal the inheritance and the title of the Marquess of Haleston from the Earl of Scartmoor, an older gentleman who, she'd heard from some of the servants, was a disagreeable soul, but one who'd had a rather tragic life. He had apparently disowned his only daughter when she married a commoner, a decision which his wife never forgave him for, but which, alas, he was too stubborn to reverse. His beloved wife had subsequently died, and he had become a joyless, reclusive man. According to his servants, the Earl was actually very kind to them, and they protected him and served him with pleasure, but the peers of society found him distasteful, no doubt because he did not comply with their expectations of his position.

She had been horrified at what the Baron planned, but it had only hardened the resolve that she had already made, to do whatever it took to get herself out of this terrible position, and, if possible, cause the Baron's plans to fail. What he wanted to do was not right, in any way, for it subverted the law, and the rules of society, as well as depriving a man of what was rightfully his. Once Kitty had heard their voices cease and footsteps recede, she had slipped out from behind the heavy velvet drapes and moved to leave the study, only to collide with Herbert who was returning to the room.

"Hmph! What the…,"

"Excuse me, Mr Calthorpe," said Kitty, trying to recover. "Jane wanted her stuffed bear, or she would not be able to sleep."

"Where were you just now?"

"I've just come now to collect the bear."

Her heart had pounded with fear, and she had shrunk back from him, not liking the look in his eyes at all.

"You did not just arrive, I would have seen you," he said. "You were eavesdropping, you ungrateful slip of muslin."

He grabbed her wrist and twisted it.

"No, sir, I swear, I only wanted the bear."

She had been sobbing by then, from fear, and the pain of his grasp on her.

"You were here for my stepfather, admit it. I see the way he looks at you. You've been giving him favours and disgracing my mother's memory." Herbert had pulled her arm up behind her and held her tighter, dragging her against him so that she could sense his hot breath on her neck. "I want some of what you've been giving him."

"No!"

He had slackened his grip on her as he reached down to release himself from his breeches and, in a single swift move, she had spun in his grasp, raised her knee sharply between his legs, then twisted away and run from the room, while Herbert doubled over in pain, groaning.

"I'll make you pay!"

She'd heard his shout as she'd retreated up the staircase to Jane's room, out of breath as she reached the top.

The following weeks were unbearable for Kitty as she now had two men to avoid. She had also feared that Herbert would tell his stepfather that he'd caught her eavesdropping in his study. Luckily, he seemed to have forgotten all about it, distracted when news came of the death of the Marquess of Haleston.

For, in those intervening weeks, Herbert and the Baron had often been huddled together in the study, working on some documents, carefully created on sheets of very old parchment. She was sure that they were forging a letter or other document of some kind, to support their intended deception – and now, they would use those documents to attempt to claim what was not theirs. The Baron had been speaking, in the hearing of the servants, of the 'surprising old documents he had found, amongst his father's old papers', which were about to change his fortunes. So, at the news of the death of the Marquess, Baron Reville's household was immediately thrown into a frenzy of preparation as the family and servants alike started speaking of the Baron's forthcoming title.

Kitty had not been able to bear to think that the deception they planned might work. These two conniving men were not, she'd felt, worthy of such a title. Although she had known that she would lose her governess position and be out on the streets for what she was about to do, she had made a decision. Having no idea how she would be received, she had gone directly to the Earl of Scartmoor's townhouse in London and asked to see the Earl about a vitally important matter. To her surprise, after she was told to wait in the foyer, the butler returned barely ten minutes later and led her through to meet the Earl.

She had soon learned that her apprehension was unfounded, and that the Earl was a kind and gentle man, although the mistakes of his tragic past had weighed heavily on him, and he was painfully unhappy. At first he had no interest in challenging Baron Reville for the title of Marquess which was rightfully his, but he was smitten with the young woman who seemed to only want what was his fair right to be realised, with no concern for how it may adversely affect her. But then, as they had discussed what the Baron had planned, the Earl realised that, should Reville succeed, he would gain not only the Haleston title, but the Scartmoor one as well, by dispossessing the Earl's father from the line of succession. The Marquess had regarded Kitty with a pained expression before making a statement on the matter.

"I have never found it in me to like my nephew. But now – that he would dishonour the family so – I cannot allow it, cannot allow everything that I have built to go to him, in such a manner. Nor can I allow him to deprive my son of what is rightfully his – no matter that my son will not speak to me, for he blames me for my wife's death, from sorrow at never seeing our daughter again."

By the end of the month, the Earl of Scartmoor had been confirmed to the title of Marquess of Haleston, and inherited several grand entailed properties in the process, and Kitty had become his wife. The College of Arms, upon being called in to resolve the matter of the dispute brought by the Baron, had quickly declared the documents the Baron presented to be forgeries, and had dismissed the Baron's claim.

Herbert had initially tried to ruin Kitty by announcing to anyone who would listen that she was a commoner who had tricked the Marquess into marriage for his money and titles. But the new Marquess had made certain that the Baron Reville and Herbert would never speak ill of her, by forging an agreement whereby, in exchange, he would not expose the deception which they had tried to perpetrate – although some gossip still leaked out, and the *ton* spoke of it in whispers, wondering if the tale was true.

In the years which followed, Kitty doted on her elderly husband, whom she truly grew to love. After he had an apoplexy which left part of his face distorted, she had cared for him night and day, insisting on serving him his meals herself and walking with him in the garden when he was able to do so. Although he remained somewhat reclusive and had never fully recovered from the apoplexy, nor from his heartbreak over the death of his first wife and the loss of his daughter, he credited Kitty with making his twilight years comfortable and enjoyable, especially once she had managed to bring about a reconciliation between the Marquess and his son.

Kitty and Annabelle had become fast friends during Annabelle's weekly visits to her uncle, given that the Marquess' niece and his wife were similar in age. When Hannah wrote to Annabelle and asked for a reference to help her, following the death of her stepfather, Kitty had gently told her husband that he had a granddaughter. She had vowed to do whatever she could to protect the girl and see that she would be taken care of.

✶✶✶✶✶

Hannah could barely drink her tea as she absorbed the extraordinary story. Occasionally, she would gaze through the window to look at her grandfather, expecting him to disappear at any moment. But there he sat, with the blanket over his lap, sometimes dozing with his eyes closed and head bowed, then waking and raising his head to the sun to feel the warmth on his skin, or cocking his head as if to listen for the sound of some forgotten voice in the distance.

"We should be getting home, Hannah, would you like to tell your grandfather that you are leaving?"

Annabelle's voice was gentle, as if she knew that Hannah's thoughts were still tangled.

During her recitation of events over the past hours, Kitty had explained that the Marquess was fully aware of Hannah's betrothal - as well as her misgivings and concerns about the reasons for Lord Tarynholt's proposal. In fact, since Hannah's parents were both deceased, Lord Tarynholt had felt it right to ask the Marquess for permission to marry her.

As Hannah said her final goodbyes, and the Marquess wished her well on her wedding day, which he said he did not feel fit enough to attend, he appeared to sense the lingering doubts behind her sombre eyes. He reached for her hands and urged her to sit beside him for a moment.

"My dear granddaughter," he began. "I am an old fool and do not expect you to believe anything which I say, because my mistakes have likely caused you much pain during your life. But there is one thing of which I am sure." He started to cough, and as a cool breeze fluttered through the garden he pulled the blanket closer around his knees. "When your Lord Tarynholt asked my permission to marry you, there was only one reason I gave him my consent."

"What was that, grandfather?"

"The look of love in his eyes," said the Marquess simply. "I recognised the same look in Lord Tarynholt's eyes that I saw in the eyes of Charles Browning more than twenty years ago, when he asked my permission to marry your mother, and I denied him. I denied him because I did not think he was good enough to be her husband. And I was so very wrong."

Tears sprang to Hannah's eyes as she thought of her parents, whom she missed terribly.

"They were happy, grandfather."

"I know. And I have regretted my actions for all of these years. Although, I cannot entirely regret what happened – for if Eleanor had not married the Duke, then you would not exist, and I cannot regret your existence. I am glad that you spent so many years growing up, thinking of Browning as your father. He obviously did well by you, no matter that you were not a child of his body, and I am grateful for that. Neither you nor Lord Tarynholt need my permission to marry, for you have your majority. You must make your own decision. But he loves you, Hannah, of that I am certain. Be happy." Kitty had come into the garden as she sensed that the coolness of the air was starting to distress her husband. "Now I must go indoors and rest, my dear," he said softly, "come back and see me again soon, if you will."

Robert had found himself more and more concerned, as the day of his wedding approached. No matter what he had said, Hannah still did not seem to believe that he spoke the truth when he declared his feelings for her.

Then, just this morning, he had called upon her, to find that something had changed. She had been sitting in the parlour at Lady Deerwood's, a tea tray before her, when he arrived. She looked, if it was possible, even more beautiful than usual, and his heart ached to think that she might never forgive him. But she had lifted her eyes to his, and risen to greet him with a smile.

"My Lord, tell me the truth. I will hear the words from you again, and I will permit myself to trust that you speak the truth – for I cannot go forward forever doubting. The events of the last few days have reminded me that people can change, that people can make mistakes, and recover from them. I have not been fair to you, by judging you on one circumstance."

He had stepped up to her, and taken her hands in his.

"Hannah, my darling Hannah, I love you. I believe that you captured my heart on the very first day that I saw you, even though I did not realise it at the time. Can you forgive me for my foolishness in not declaring myself from the beginning?"

Her soft blue eyes had studied him as she spoke, and then her fingers had pressed his.

"I can. Robert... I love you, also."

At that, he had bent and kissed her, a soft promise for the future.

Chapter Ten

"Hannah, you were an absolutely beautiful bride."

Kitty was the first to congratulate them as they made their way out of the church. She and Robert had been married just a few moments earlier, and the number of well-wishers who had come to show their support for the couple was extraordinary. Hannah was rather overwhelmed by it all, but inside, the happiness at having married the man she had come to love was enough to make her feel that she could cope with anything.

"Why are there so many people in attendance?"

Hannah whispered the question to Robert as they went towards the waiting carriage.

"Everyone wanted to see the bride who captured my heart."

Beside her, Robert was beaming as he said it, and she blushed at his words.

"Ahoy!"

They both turned toward the cry and were thrilled to spot Lord Marlby in the crowd, making his way forward to congratulate them.

"It's about time you made your way back to London, Marlby!"

Robert grinned at his friend, and beside him, Hannah was even more anxious to see Lord Marlby than Robert was. As they moved closer to the carriage, Lord Marlby walking beside them, she immediately asked the question which was closest to her heart.

"Have you any news of the orphanage?"

Robert had been evasive during the past week when she'd tried to ask him what progress he'd made in seeing to the orphans' welfare, only telling her that his man of business would deal with it, and she would be advised as soon as a solution was found.

Lord Marlby's smile faded, as did his hope that he could avoid this delicate subject with Hannah, today of all days. He bowed his head before breaking the news to her.

"I'm afraid that I come with bad news. I stopped at the manor, but the orphans were no longer there."

He glanced at Robert, who shot daggers at him with his eyes for delivering such distressing news to his bride on their wedding day. But Hannah barely noticed that exchange, so taken aback was she by what he had said.

"What?" She tried unsuccessfully to control a sob. "Did you locate the vicar and ask where they went?"

Marlby nodded.

"A most uncooperative fellow. He was not at all inclined to speak with me regarding the orphans, or their whereabouts. I was simply informed that they had left the manor some weeks earlier, as he and his family had need of the entire house. He declared that he did not know where they had planned to relocate to."

"He evicted them! Oh, I was afraid that might happen…"

"I am so sorry, my Lady. My own travels were delayed, and I fear that I reached Lower Nettlefold later than I had anticipated. Perhaps if I had passed by sooner…"

"No, it is not your fault."

"Nonetheless, I wish…"

Hannah ignored his protestations and turned her gaze to her husband.

"You promised me, more than a month ago, that you would take care of them immediately! I trusted you."

Hannah tried to control her emotions, considering that several of the wedding onlookers were still nearby. Robert was urging her to step into the carriage, and she went willingly, suddenly unable to bear being in public view.

"Hannah, I promised you that I would provide for the orphans and that is exactly what I shall do. I am certain that my man of business will be able to inquire with the villagers and locate them."

"The poor darlings. And what of Mrs Bell and Mrs Willis? Their well-being is just as dependent on there being a funded orphanage as the children's is. Their life's work has been in caring for those children. My father would be so disappointed in me to know that I have not protected all of them."

She settled onto the seat beside him, and, as the carriage door shut behind them, she could no longer hold back the sob.

However, despite her distress and concern for the orphans, it was impossible for Hannah to stay angry with her husband. As the carriage took them to Tarynholt House – her new home - she leant into the curve of his arm, and they spoke quietly about how unfortunate the timing had been that both Lord Marlby and Robert's man of business must have just missed reaching the children and their caretakers before they had to move.

Robert promised her, again, that he would find the orphans, and make everything right, then kissed her with gentle care.

She sighed, and made the choice to trust his word – at least for now.

They spent their wedding night in their London townhouse.

Robert was charming, flirtatious, and gentle and Hannah was unable to hide her desire for her husband, or resist the touch which sent shivers up her spine. She felt like the luckiest woman in the world, to have found a man she desired, and who treated her with gentle care and respect.

Even though it meant little sleep, they were both anxious to be on the road early the following morning, for the journey to his estate near Bath — the estate where his mother had spent the last years of her life, and where he had spent his happiest years - would take either a single very long day, or two days, depending on the weather. It was but a week to Easter, and Hannah wanted to have the chance to search the area for the orphans for at least a few days before Easter was upon them. She was glad that the estate where Robert wished to live was relatively close to Lower Nettlefold, for it would make things far easier, and she would be glad to see familiar terrain.

Robert had vowed to Hannah that his first order of business when they reached the country was to send ten men, if needed, to find the orphans. Hannah believed him, and trusted that he would not let her down again.

She watched the various houses and buildings pass by and found herself smiling. How different this journey was to the one she had taken, coming to London only a short time ago, when she knew not what the future would hold for her.

She was now a married woman, a Countess, she had met her grandfather, and she was very likely to have a child of her own within the year. The scope of the change in her life was enormous, and she was beyond grateful for the way in which things had turned out.

*****

The weather stayed fine, and Robert, after discussing it with Hannah, chose to push on into the night, so that they would reach Nettlerush Banks after a single day's travel. It was approaching midnight when they drew to a stop on the gravel before the porticoed entrance, and Robert felt the tension leave him as the peace of this familiar and well-loved place surrounded him.

But it was only peaceful for a few minutes – then the servants detected their arrival, and there was a flurry of activity as their luggage was unloaded, and every servant came to present themselves to the new mistress of the house. Once the introductions were done, with Hannah being kind and gracious to everyone, whilst begging their indulgence if she did not, immediately, manage to remember every name, Robert turned to address his butler, Harman.

"Please have cook prepare a light supper and send it up. Please also have a bath brought up, and send a maid to assist Lady Tarynholt. You may retire after that."

Peters, Robert's valet, had already hurried upstairs, overseeing the footmen who carried the luggage.

Taking Hannah's arm, Robert ushered her up the stairs and down a long hallway to their suite of rooms. He opened the door with a flourish, and smiled as Hannah gasped.

"Oh! What a beautiful room!"

The room – a private parlour, which served as the centre of the suite, with bedroom and dressing rooms opening from it - was decorated in shades of blue and cream, the walls adorned by delicate watercolour paintings of the house and the surrounding countryside.

"Thank you – I am so glad that you like it. Of course, if there are things about any of this that you do not like, when can always change them..."

"Oh no, Robert – I would not change any of this."

"Then let me show you your dressing room. There will be a warm bath for you soon, and a maid to assist you. While you bathe, I will just check with the housekeeper that all is in good order, then I will return."

Hannah nodded, and soon, he left her in the care of a maid, so that she might wash the dust of travel from her skin. He slipped back downstairs, and found Mrs Carstairs waiting for him.

"Is everything in order, as I requested, Mrs Carstairs?"

"It is, my Lord. All has been done exactly as Mr Withers instructed."

"That is excellent to hear. I will inspect everything, with my wife, tomorrow. For now, please go to your bed. And thank you for your work on this matter."

Mrs Carstairs smiled warmly, bobbed a curtsey, and went.

For a moment, Robert simply stood there, as her footsteps receded, leaving him with no sound but the ticking of the large clock which stood to one side, and the faint call of a nightbird outside. His heart was full of joy – here he was, with everything safe from his rapacious cousin, married to a woman he loved, and able to relax, finally, far from the viper pit of London society.

He turned, and went back upstairs, stepping into their rooms quietly. As he did, the maid slipped out, bobbing him a curtsey as she went. Inside, he crossed the parlour to the bedroom door, and opened it carefully.

"Hannah…"

He allowed his voice to trail off and smiled as he saw that she had already fallen asleep. It had been a very long day on the road, and she must have been exhausted. He would take her on a tour of the house and grounds in the morning, after breakfast, and hope that everything met with her approval.

He stepped past the bed and into his own dressing room, where a yawning Peters waited to assist him, and was soon changed into his night attire. As he slipped into the bed beside his delightful wife, he thought with pleasure of the coming days.

*****

In the morning, Hannah dressed in a simple day gown, rather surprising the maid with her choice, pleased to inhale the fresh country air in comparison to the smoky air of London. A glance out of the bedroom window showed her rolling countryside and the rich greens of well-tended fields.

A short while later, she entered the breakfast room as Robert was dismissing the housekeeper with a list of instructions.

"Good morning, my dear, I trust that you slept well."

She still felt slightly worn from the long journey in the carriage, but was happy and beginning to be hungry.

"I did – I do apologise for falling asleep before you came back upstairs."

He smiled at her, his expression bright.

"That is not a problem my dear – yesterday was a very long day indeed. I hope it will be all right with you if I show you around the estate immediately after breakfast. It is Easter in only a few days, and I hoped that you would agree that we should plan an egg hunt on the grounds for the village children."

Hannah felt as though she'd been kicked in the stomach. She and Mrs Bell had spoken of their plans for Easter with the children of the orphanage. She did not want to seem ungrateful for the beautiful home which she would now be sharing with her wonderful husband, but neither could she ease the pang of guilt which gripped her as she thought of the orphans. She forced herself to maintain a calm expression as she replied.

"Yes, of course, my Lord."

As she spoke, she knew that she had answered too formally and in a manner lacking enthusiasm. But Robert seemed to accept it without concern. They sat, and she found that her appetite was severely reduced, so she ate but a few mouthfuls of toast and marmalade. When they rose from the table, Robert took her hand and slipped it into the crook of his arm.

"I would like to give you a wedding gift."

Hannah looked at him, rather startled, wondering what that statement had to do with a tour of the grounds. But he said nothing more, and simply led her from the house, out into the crisp morning air and across the dewy grass of a vast lawn. It was beautiful, and despite her sadness about the orphans, she could not help but appreciate it, despite the fact that the hem of her dress was becoming damp with the dew.

They walked on in companionable silence, but Hannah's curiosity grew, the further they went. What gift could he possibly wish to give her, which required walking across the countryside like this?

She looked around and tried to take in the scale of the vast estate and rolling hills surrounding it. It seemed to go on for miles, and she wondered where the boundaries of the estate might be, amongst all of those fields and forests. After a stroll of perhaps ten minutes, across lawns and then down a lane bordered by stone walls and hedges, they reached a long stone building with a wooden staircase leading to a large open verandah.

"What is this building?"

She feigned interest, although she was ready to return to their home, and now regretted eating so little for breakfast, as the brisk walk had raised her appetite again. Then the front door was flung open, and before Hannah could grasp what was happening, a sea of smiling faces poured out through that door, ran down the stairs and raced to her.

Within seconds, she was surrounded by children, their arms wrapped around her legs and faces buried in her skirts.

"Hannah, Hannah, we missed you!"

The orphans! Happiness filled her, and she tried to hug all of them at once.

She looked up to see Mrs Bell and Mrs Willis on the verandah, the two women unable to contain their tears.

*****

Easter was a flurry of activity.

Mrs Bell made Hannah's favourite hot cross buns on Good Friday, after which they showed all of the children how to dye the eggs and decorate them for the egg hunt the following day. In addition to the orphans, the village children would attend the egg hunt at the estate, and Hannah was looking forward to hearing the giggles and laughter of children once again. She had missed that in London.

She had forgiven Robert for keeping the fact that he had been the one to move the orphans from the vicarage manor in Lower Nettlefold secret from her. He had wanted it to be a delightful wedding surprise and had not anticipated that Lord Marlby would report to Hannah that they were missing.

Mrs Willis reminded Hannah that eggs were associated with rebirth and fertility and new beginnings. She winked at Hannah, who blushed at what the widow was implying.

Once the children had settled down for the evening, the three women sewed pastel-coloured bonnets for all of the girls to wear on Easter morning. By the time they had finished, Hannah was exhausted, but overwhelmingly happy.

*****

"I thought you'd never come to bed," Robert said, pretend pouting at his bride. "I suspect that I shall have to compete for your attention now."

"Never fear, my love," she said. "I will always have time for you. We may have been brought together by your father's Will, but I can't find it in me to object to that now… Instead, I can see that ensuring that you have an heir might be the most pleasant thing I've ever done…"

He laughed, and Hannah smiled as she wrapped her arms around her husband's neck and kissed him deeply. Robert slipped one arm under her legs to easily lift her up and carry her to the bed, all the while continuing the kiss.

Epilogue

The leaves were changing from green to vibrant shades of yellow, orange, and red and Robert was anxious to return to Hannah following a trip to London to deal with business.

She had not joined him because she had been feeling tired and nauseous for several days before his departure – and he was hoping that it was actually a foreshadowing of good news. If she was with child, he would be delighted – and he promised himself that, as a father, he would be everything that his own father had not been.

He was also bearing news from London for her.

Kitty had reported that Annabelle had, to her delight, delivered a healthy baby girl a few weeks earlier, and Kitty was going to the country to keep her company and assist her for the coming months.

Hannah's grandfather, the Marquess of Haleston, had gone to God, passing quietly in his sleep, the night that Annabelle was delivered of her daughter. Robert had called on him that very day and reported that Hannah was thriving and looking forward to a London visit in the spring. It seemed that knowing all was well with her had settled the old man's mind at the end.

Robert knew that Hannah would be saddened to learn that she would not see her grandfather again. Kitty had assured him that her husband had died peacefully, knowing that his granddaughter was happy, healthy and loved.

The Marquess' son had been with him, the last distance between them repaired, and would take on the title honourably. Now, as the carriage turned down the long drive into Nettlerush Banks, Robert watched the golden falling leaves, and thought of the new growth which would replace them in the spring.

So much had changed in his life, in a few short months – he had found peace, he had found happiness, and he had found love. What more could a man want?

Only a kiss from his beautiful wife...

The End.

I hope that you enjoyed 'To Wed an Earl'

**You'll find a preview of another of my books,
'The Duke and the Spinster'
just after the
'About the Author'
section of this book.**

About the Author

Arietta Richmond has been a compulsive reader and writer all her life. Whilst her reading has covered an enormous range of topics, history has always fascinated her, and historical novels have been amongst her favourite reading.

She has written a wide range of work, from business articles and other non-fiction works (published under a pen name) but fiction has always been a major part of her life. Now, her Regency Historical Romance books are finally being released. The Derbyshire Set is comprised of 11 novels (9 released so far). The 'His Majesty's Hounds' series is comprised of 17 novels, with the last now released.

She also has a number of standalone novels released, and four other series of novels in development. She lives in Australia, and when not reading or writing, likes to travel, and to see in person the places where history happened.

Be the first to know about it when Arietta's next book is released! Sign up to Arietta's newsletter at

http://www.ariettarichmond.com

When you do, you will receive two free subscriber exclusive books - **'A Gift of Love',** which is a prequel to the Derbyshire Set series, and ends on the day that 'The Earl's Unexpected Bride' begins, and **'Madame's Christmas Marquis'** which is an additional story in the His Majesty's Hounds series.

These stories are not for sale anywhere – they are absolutely exclusive to newsletter subscribers!

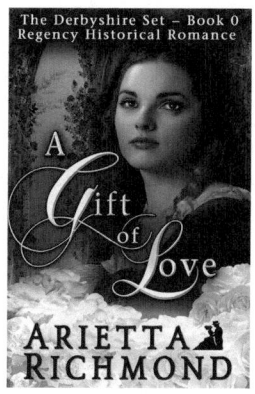 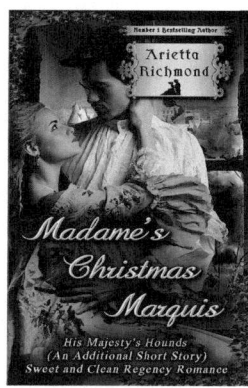

Connect with Arietta:

Donate and support her on Kofi.com
https://ko-fi.com/ariettarichmondauthor
Follow her on Amazon –
https://www.amazon.com/Arietta-Richmond/e/B016GG1KJ6/
Like her Facebook Page –
https://www.facebook.com/AriettaRichmondAuthor
Follow her on Twitter –
https://twitter.com/AriettaRichmond
Follow her on Instagram –
https://www.instagram.com/AriettaRichmond/
Follow her on Bookbub –
https://www.bookbub.com/authors/arietta-richmond
Follow her on Goodreads –
https://www.goodreads.com/author/show/14508806.Arietta_Richmond

Here is your preview of

The Duke and The Spinster

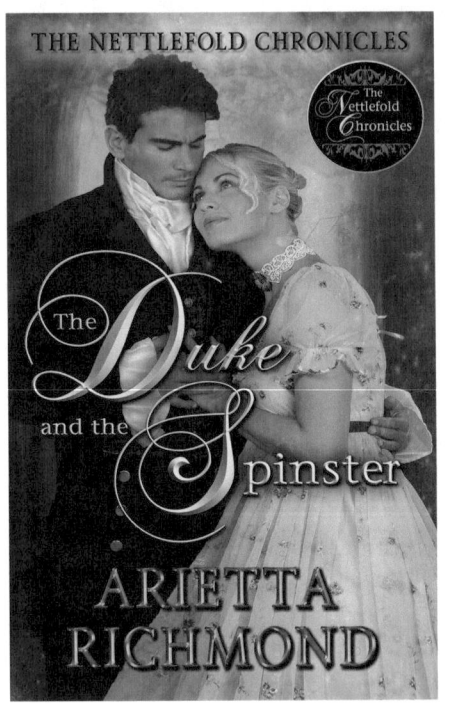

Clean Regency Romance

Arietta Richmond

Chapter One

"Really Garrett, you are just avoiding the matter! You can't put it off indefinitely!"

The door shut solidly – not quite slammed, but close.

Garrett Rutherford, the Duke of Kilmerstan, stared gloomily at his near empty brandy glass. Above him on the wall, the portraits of his father and his grandfather, looked down upon him. He felt their disapproval keenly.

His mother was, of course, right – not that he liked to admit it. He could not avoid marriage forever, not if the title was to have an heir – for his cousin, Lord Giles Fortnum, would make a terrible Duke, and Garrett had no intention of allowing him to remain next in line for the title. But the eligible women available amongst the right strata of society were enough to make a man feel ill.

He was beyond tired of being hunted by them, as if he could be caught and manipulated into choosing a Duchess. The harder they tried, the more he resisted. He had come to despise social occasions, and had hoped that, upon retiring to Kilmerstan Castle for the summer, he might largely avoid them. That assumption was proving irritatingly wrong.

First, there had been the invitation, a few weeks past, to an occasion of sorts to welcome Viscount Mooresfield home. He had chosen not to attend, and was grateful for it, for, by all reports, the evening had degenerated into a shouting match between Mooresfield and the Earl of Banfield – an unpleasant man at the best of times, and one who Garrett was particularly displeased with, as he had been attempting to court Garrett's sister Isabelle for some months. Anything that Garrett could do to break that association, he would.

And now, an invitation to another event at Hallingbrook Grange – one which seemed to have some hope of being of a more genteel and appropriate nature, but which still did not appeal at all. For Mooresfield had disappeared, to London he believed, for a week after the last event to much gossip and speculation. And then, not long after his return, had announced, to everyone's surprise, his betrothal to Marianne Jones, the Baker's daughter!

He knew that Mooresfield had never been very concerned with status, having spent most of his life as a third son, and never expecting to inherit, but still! Marianne was a nice enough girl, but *the ton* would crucify the man for choosing a commoner with such a background. He could imagine the gossip that must already be circulating.

This latest invitation was to a week-long house party, in celebration of that betrothal. The guest list, as discovered by his mother, was extensive.

He had to assume that summer boredom was responsible for so many of substance attending – or perhaps the spreading gossip meant that they all simply wanted to see the baker's daughter who had captured the heart of a Viscount. Oddly enough, Isabelle had not seemed enthused at all, even though she normally loved social events. Regardless, his mother had almost begun to salivate at sight of the names of all of the eligible women who would be present.

Garrett knew when he was fighting a losing battle – he would have to attend, at least some of the activities – thank God he lived close enough to not have to stay at Hallingbrook!

But his mother would not allow him to escape this – the Duchess was a force to be reckoned with, when she had set her heart on something.

Of course, if he attended, he would almost certainly see Lady Prudence. Lady Prudence Baggington was the bane of his life. She had decided some years before that she was destined to marry Garrett – and had thrown herself in his path at every opportunity since, even whilst he was still in mourning for his father, and his brother. She was the most irritating woman he had ever met.

He swallowed the last of the brandy, and deposited the glass on a side table. Perhaps a brisk ride in the summer twilight would improve his mood.

✳✳✳✳✳

Lady Juliana Willoughby stared out of the window as the coach bumped over the last miles of the road to Upper Nettlefold.

The Nettlerush River ran beside the road, and the scenery was rather pretty, with the summer flowers and the green grass. She would have enjoyed visiting such a pretty place, had they been visiting for any other reason.

"Aren't you excited, Juliana? We're nearly there!"

Eleanor's voice was light, musical, and always full of delight in the world. Juliana, as always, felt the contrast between her, and her sister, acutely. She sighed, and leant back against the padded seat as they bounced over another rut in the road.

"I have nothing to be particularly excited about, Eleanor, although I will admit that the scenery is pretty. This visit is, after all, primarily for your benefit."

"Oh, don't be so gloomy, Juliana – I am sure that you will meet some interesting and eligible men as well. There will even be a Duke present – an *unmarried* Duke!"

"Who will, undoubtedly, not even notice my existence. You, however, are far more likely to be noticed."

"Don't be so silly Juliana – I am sure that you will be noticed."

Juliana sighed again, shaking her head. Their mother, used to this type of conversation, decided to distract them. Their father, as always on long journeys, was propped against the corner of the seat, and gently snoring.

"Girls! Must you have this conversation over and over? Eleanor – Juliana is older – why she's nearly a spinster by most people's accounting, and it stands to reason that you, at nineteen, and pretty as you are, will get more attention. Just accept it, and concentrate on finding yourself a husband – preferably a wealthy one."

Eleanor nodded, with a sidelong glance at Juliana, and began to discuss with their mother who might be in attendance. Juliana kept the gentle smile fixed on her face, and went back to watching the world go by outside the window. Her eyes pricked with pointless tears, but she repressed them ruthlessly. By now, she should be used to it.

Being a spinster was infinitely preferable to being a clumsy, inelegant, too tall, too old woman amongst the glittering parade of young beauties. The tongues of the gossips of the ton were cruel. She'd had enough of their edge three years ago, and had avoided society as much as possible since.

Soon, they rumbled over an old stone bridge, the river rushing beneath, and the road took them into a large open square in the centre of the town of Upper Nettlefold. At one end of the square stood their destination – Hardcastle House.

It was a large building, which had once been an elegant manor, and now had been converted into a boarding house for the upper classes, a summer retreat for those who could not afford the prices in nearby Bath, or who were attending an overfull house party at one of the surrounding estates.

Which was exactly their situation. Funds were tight, for her father still had not managed to entirely repair the damage which his father had done to their estates and their wealth. And the house party at Hallingbrook Grange had overflowed to here, and to the two Inns.

Her father had drawn the line at the idea of them staying in even a higher-class Inn, but had accepted the boarding house as a necessity.

Their driver turned into the narrow arch through the building and pulled to a halt in the courtyard within. Soon, Juliana stood in the warm summer sun, watching as footmen rushed out to unload their belongings, and a stablehand came out to show their coachman where the vehicle and horses were to be housed. The bustle was pleasant, and mildly interesting to observe – far different from their stableyard at home.

"Come girls, let us go inside, away from all of this dust and dirt – your father can deal with the arrangements here for now."

Juliana and Eleanor followed their mother dutifully, but Juliana cast a longing glance back outside – perhaps there was a garden, somewhere, where she might sit and read in the sun. The slight chill of the building closed around her, and she turned her attention to the woman who came forward to meet them.

"Good afternoon, my Lady – am I correct in the assumption that you are the Countess of Delbarton?"

"That is correct. Mrs Hardcastle, I presume?"

"Yes – and these must be your charming daughters."

"Indeed. This is Lady Juliana, and this is Lady Eleanor. The Earl will be here in a moment – he is just directing the footmen who are dealing with our baggage. Our maid and his valet will be along in the other carriage shortly."

"Excellent. Do let me show you to your suite of rooms, and then I'll get some tea sent up. You must all be fatigued after your journey."

They nodded, gratefully, and followed her up the stairs.

Chapter Two

Juliana was pleased when her mother chose a quiet spot on the edges of the ballroom at Hallingbrook Grange, where a couch and two chairs provided enough seating for them all. The potted palms and the draperies which also filled the edges of the alcove gave her some hope of remaining inconspicuous. Eleanor saw things completely differently.

"Oh Mother! I know that having seats is a good idea, but here? In this dingy corner? How will any of the gentlemen even notice me here?"

"Don't fuss, Eleanor. We will move about the room for a time, meeting others that we may know – although there are precious few here that we do know. At least there are enough that we will be able to obtain introductions as needed. And this does mean that there are many eligible gentlemen here that have not seen you before…"

Eleanor stopped, struck by the significance of her mother's words, then turned to study, more closely, the people filling the room.

Juliana was also studying them, but for completely different reasons. She found people fascinating if she did not have to interact with them. Their mannerisms and movements gave away so much about their thoughts and their personalities.

It was only when she had to speak to them, or, heaven forbid, dance with them, that she wished herself anywhere else but there. If a gentleman spoke to her, she became, in her own mind, instantly as she had been three years before, when she had stumbled through dances, tripped over her own feet, and embarrassed herself in every way imaginable. Her first Season had been her last, by her own choice – she never wished to expose herself to feeling like that again. It did not matter that she had spent the three years since being intensely careful about how she stood, how she moved, how she spoke – the second that a man addressed her, all of that fell away, and she was the gawky clumsy, too tall girl again.

Her father, aware of how Juliana usually approached the world, began to quietly inform her of who was who. Most of the wealthy and titled people from the local area were there - the Earl of Rothlyn, the Marquess of Westwood, Baron Torsford, Viscount Mooresfield – whose house this was – and Mr William Allgood. Notably absent was the Duke of Kilmerstan – Eleanor would be disappointed if he did not appear for the evening. The Ball was the official start of the long house party, and was quite the glittering event.

There were others of significance, drawn from Bath, and even as far away as London. Her father did not know them all by name, but their dress and manner marked them out as of the nobility. Juliana studied them all carefully, amused by the posturing of the newly rich.

Even amongst the wealthy and titled, there were layers in society – layers that were quite visible, as people interacted – or chose not to. Layers in which Juliana's family were, despite the title, rather close to the bottom, for they were by no means fabulously wealthy.

Eleanor and Lady Delbarton moved off into the room, circulating amongst the guests, garnering introductions. Soon, as was to be expected, Eleanor was surrounded by a cluster of hopeful young men. Juliana marvelled at how easily Eleanor dealt with it, how happy, how graceful she seemed, no matter what. She envied her that ability, oh, so much!

Turning her eyes away from Eleanor, suddenly unable to stand watching it, she looked to the door where Viscount Mooresfield stood, welcoming arriving guests. He had just finished speaking to a gentleman who turned to move into the room as the next guest stepped up to the host.

Juliana became completely still. He was striking – tall, very dark hair, a lean hard body, well displayed by perfectly tailored clothes, and a handsome face, with strong, almost severe lines to it. There was nothing of the fop or dandy about this man. Plain colours and simple elegance made him stand out far more than any amount of ostentation could. And he moved with the kind of fluid, controlled smoothness that Juliana longed to be able to emulate.

For the first time in a very long time, Juliana was gazing at a man she found undeniably attractive. It was a rather disturbing thing to realise.

"Ah, Juliana – see, over there by the door – the Duke of Kilmerstan has made his appearance."

Her father's voice broke the spell the new arrival had cast upon her, and she turned, looking as casually unconcerned as possible.

"Oh? That's the Duke? I'm sure that Eleanor will be thrilled. He's rather... severe looking, isn't he?"

"By all accounts, most women find him attractive. He's unmarried, but the gossips say he'll be looking for a wife soon, for his only heir is a distant cousin that, it's said, he doesn't like. His brother was killed in France, and he's two sisters to find husbands for, so he'll be a busy man for the next few years."

Her father chuckled, amused by the fact that, no matter a man's title, some things remained the same – finding husbands for young ladies was a daunting task.

Juliana turned back to studying the room, finding her eyes drawn to the Duke, inescapably. He had greeted various people, then stopped to talk to Baron Torsford. The eyes of most of the young women in the room were on him, and it seemed obvious that they were all hoping for his attention.

One rather determined looking woman was moving in his direction. She was a little solidly built, and dressed in the height of fashion, as far as style, but in such a terrible combination of colours and patterns that Juliana felt ill at the sight.

Observing the manoeuvring that would undoubtedly occur throughout the evening should be amusing indeed. She settled in to simply watch, quite confident that, if she stayed quietly trucked away, no-one would ask her to dance.

✳✳✳✳✳

Garrett had forced himself to regard the Ball at Hallingbrook Grange as potentially interesting, when his first instinct was to avoid it completely. Isabelle and Eugenia were full of enthusiasm, and his mother was determined that they took the opportunity to meet potential suitors. Apparently, there were eligible gentlemen coming from London, and Bath.

Upon arrival at the Grange, his mother and sisters had almost immediately disappeared into the crush of people, seeking out friends to chatter with, and to leverage for introductions, leaving him to greet George, Viscount Mooresfield, at the door.

"Good evening. I must apologise for my mother and sisters somewhat unseemly haste. It appears that the lure of gossip is greater than that of ordinary conversation."

"Your Grace, it's good to see you here tonight. And as for gossip… I'm sure that your presence will set off a cascade of hope in the hearts of the unmarried ladies here, who will then discuss you incessantly. I have recently come to realise that the benefits of being betrothed are manifold, and one of those benefits is no longer being the subject of that kind of discussion and attention."

Garrett laughed, and gently clapped the Viscount on the shoulder.

"Yes, congratulations. I hope that you'll be happy. Although... I doubt you're done with gossip, for, by marrying the baker's daughter, you've given them plenty to whisper about, haven't you?"

"Very true, very true. But I shall weather the storm."

They spoke a moment more, then Garrett moved away into the room. People greeted him as he slipped through the crowds, and he could feel the eyes of the women upon him – the mothers who wanted their daughters to be a Duchess, and the daughters who craved the title. He doubted that one in twenty of them cared at all about him as a man. Although he was equally sure that they were pleased that he was young, and not ill favoured.

He spotted Torsford and moved towards him. They had been at Eton together, and the man was as close as he had to a friend amongst the local nobility, although of late Torsford's house parties had been drawing the wrong set. It was disturbing to see him entangled with the rakes, gamblers, and wastrels of the *ton*. Tonight, Torsford seemed in a better mood, and they spoke of the new Irish Hunter he had purchased, and his plans for his estate. Garrett carefully avoided meeting the eye of any of the young women, no matter how much they tried to attract his attention. He expected that he would, by evening's end, be forced to dance, but he would avoid that also as long as possible.

He scanned the room, checking who was present, and assessing the likelihood of having to deal with people he found annoying. As he did, a most unwelcome sight greeted him. Lady Prudence Baggington, headed in his direction. She was unmistakeable - her gown, as always, well cut, in a most fashionable style that displayed her ample assets well, but made from a fabric of a pattern and colour as strident and grating to the eye as her voice was to the ear. It was enough to give a man a headache. Lady Prudence almost towed her mother, Viscountess Mortel, across the floor.

He sighed, and Torsford glanced past him, then grinned.

"Ah, the baggage has seen you. You're doomed, old man, you know that she thinks she's fated to be with you, or some such rubbish."

"I know it all too well. I must escape her somehow, or I'll be forced to dance with her."

Garrett shuddered, and Torsford laughed again, completely lacking in sympathy. Lady Prudence's pursuit of Garrett was rather a joke amongst the local nobility. But it was too late for escape – Lady Prudence and Lady Mortel were upon them.

"Good evening, Your Grace, so delightful to see you here! And your sisters too – we haven't seen enough of you, this last few years."

Garrett looked at her, and swallowed, trying not to breathe too deeply, for her choice of scents was as aggressive and tasteless as her choice of fabrics.

"Well, mourning does rather limit one's socialising."

His tone was dry, and he was looking desperately for a way to end the conversation rapidly.

"It does, it does. Still, you're past that now, aren't you? Time to move on with your life."

Lady Mortel looked significantly at her daughter as she spoke, and Garrett forced himself not to visibly flinch.

"Indeed. And the first part of that will be giving my sisters the Season they missed." Garrett saw a chance, and looked to the drapes near the terrace doors, pretending to see someone. "And it seems my sister wants me now. Do excuse me."

He turned and fled, feeling Torsford's amused eyes upon him as he did. But at least the man had the decency to continue the conversation with Lady Prudence and her mother, forcing them to stay and talk, out of politeness.

Garrett slipped out onto the terrace with a sense of relief, the slightly cool air of evening clearing the last of Lady Prudence's terrible perfume from his nostrils. He moved to the end of the terrace, into the dark shadowed area past the windows, and stood, leaning back against the rail, the scent of the riot of summer roses in the garden below surrounding him.

As he stood, a door opened at the far end of the terrace, and a woman stepped through. The light from the open door briefly showed him a tall, elegant figure, well-shaped and dressed simply in a beautiful gown of an amber shade, with hair like burnished gold coiled upon her head, a single tendril falling from it over her shoulder and drawing the eye inexorably to her décolletage.

Then the door closed, and she was just a shadow amongst shadows.

He did not move. He simply watched. Why was she out here? And why alone? Her movements were smooth, careful, and beautiful, almost like dance, as if she took precise care with every step. Everything about her was in contrast to the young women who hoped to marry him, and as opposite as could be imagined to Lady Prudence. He felt a sudden desire to meet her, to find out more.

He shook the thought aside – what kind of foolish idea was that!

Yet he moved forward, slowly, watching her and, when she slipped back into the ballroom, he also slipped in through the nearest door. Once inside, he halted, and watched her.

She went straight towards a secluded corner, and sat beside an older man and woman, and a younger girl. Her family, he supposed. Seeing her in full light, he was even more struck by her beauty, and by her self-effacing behaviour. She made no attempt to be seen, no attempt to do anything but sit quietly, unlike the other girl – her sister? – who was up again, tugging her mother after her, and off to speak to a group of women on the other side of the room. He had never before seen a beautiful woman choose to hide away in a circumstance such as this.

Intrigued, he turned away, wondering who she was. He searched the room carefully, identified the location of Lady Prudence, and was relieved to see her totally absorbed in a conversation with a collection of the more gossipy, older women. She would, hopefully, remain engaged by the gossip for some considerable time. He went in search of his mother and sisters.

Perhaps they knew who the beautiful woman in the corner was.

In the end, when he found them, he did not ask, for the thought of giving his mother the slightest hint that he found any woman interesting was terrifying. He was relieved to see that Isabelle was looking happy, and as if she was enjoying herself, for the first time since her short visit with a friend in London. He stayed with them for a short while, then sought out Mooresfield.

"Mooresfield, as the host, I make the assumption that you actually know everyone here?"

"That's perhaps rash, Kilmerstan, but why do you ask?"

"I've seen a family I can't place, and I'm curious."

"Point them out then."

Garrett did, indicating the couch and chairs in the corner, where the beautiful woman still sat, talking to the man he assumed was her father.

"Oh, yes, you wouldn't have met them. They haven't been to town the last few Seasons. Reputed to be a bit short on funds. But they're here now to, I suspect, try to marry off the younger daughter. The Earl of Delbarton, Lady Delbarton, and the two daughters. Lady Juliana and Lady Eleanor, if I remember correctly. Shall I introduce you?"

"If you would."

They moved across the room, and came to a halt before the father and daughter, who rose at their approach.

"My Lady, my Lord, may I present His Grace, the Duke of Kilmerstan?"

The woman dropped into a curtsey worthy of court and her father bowed.

"Delighted to meet you, Your Grace. I am the Earl of Delbarton, and this is my daughter, Lady Juliana."

Juliana could barely breathe. The Duke! Being introduced to her. She smiled, and hoped that her curtsey was good enough, and that he would not expect her to do more than greet him.

Across the room, Eleanor had turned, and seen what was happening. Suddenly, for the first time, she envied her sister.

Continued...

I hope that you enjoyed this preview!

Read the rest at:

https://ariettarichmond.com/go/the-duke-and-the-spinster

Books in the A Duke's Daughters – the Elbury Bouquet Series

Themed Regency Collections

Books in the His Majesty's Hounds Series

  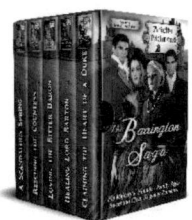

Claiming the Heart of a Duke

Intriguing the Viscount

Giving a Heart of Lace

Being Lady Harriet's Hero

Enchanting the Duke

Redeeming the Marquess

Finding the Duke's Heir

Winning the Merchant Earl

Healing Lord Barton

Kissing the Duke of Hearts

Loving the Bitter Baron

Falling for the Earl

Rescuing the Countess

Betting on a Lady's Heart

Attracting the Spymaster

Courting a Spinster for Christmas

Restoring the Earl's Honour

From Soldier Spy to Lord (Books 1 to 3 as a set)

To Love a Determined Lady (Books 4 to 6 as a set)

Love Heals a Lord (Books 7 to 9 as a set)

To Love a Dashing Lord (Books 10 to 13 as a set)

For a Lady's Honour (Books 14 to 17 as a set)

The Barrington Saga (all books related to the Barrington Family)

Books in The Derbyshire Set

The Earl's Unexpected Bride

The Captain's Compromised Heiress

The Viscount's Unsuitable Affair

The Count's Impetuous Seduction

The Rake's Unlikely Redemption

The Marquess' Scandalous Mistress

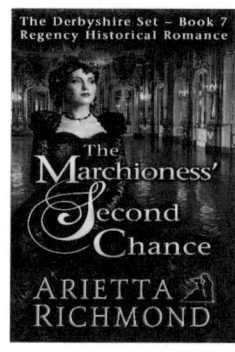  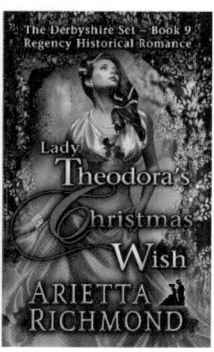

The Marchioness' Second Chance

A Viscount's Reluctant Passion

Lady Theodora's Christmas Wish

The Derbyshire Set Omnibus Edition Vol. 1 (the first three books all in one)

The Derbyshire Set Omnibus Edition Vol. 2 (the second three books all in one)

Books in the Regency Gothic Series

Lord of the Lost (Coming Soon)

Books in the Regency Scandals Series

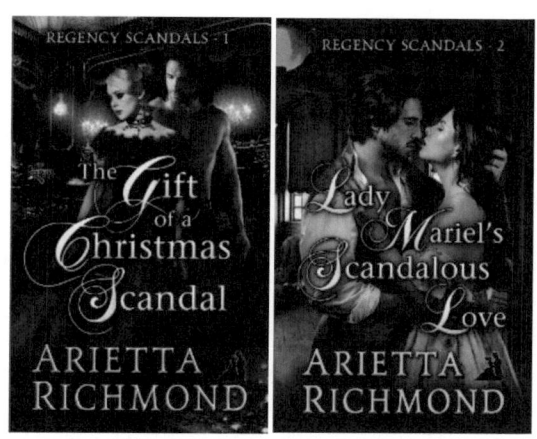

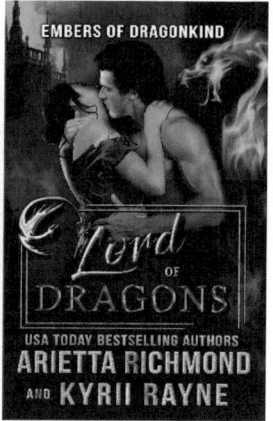

Regency Collections with Other Authors

 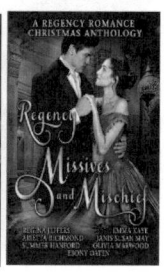

Books in the Nettlefold Chronicles

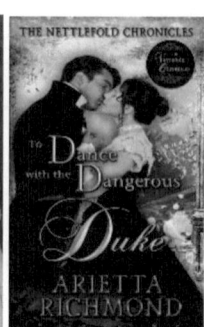

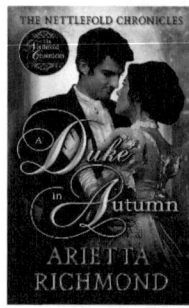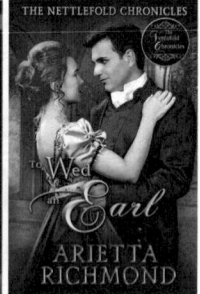

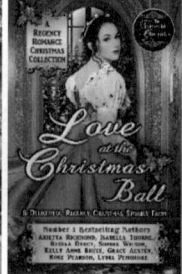

Other Books from Arietta

Other Books from Dreamstone Publishing

Dreamstone publishes books in a wide variety of categories ranging from Clean Romance to Erotica, to Kids Books, Books on Writing, Business Books, Photography, Cook Books, Diaries, Colouring books and much more. New books are released each month.

Be the first to know when our next books are coming out

Be first to get all the news – sign up for our newsletter at

http://www.dreamstonepublishing.com

Made in the USA
Thornton, CO
11/28/22 11:37:22

d03f1af7-8f40-416e-8aff-c38def8415d6R02